MW01199682

FOUR SHORT WEEKS

RETURN TO LIGHTHOUSE POINT

KAY CORRELL

ZURA LU PUBLISHING LLC

Published by Zura Lu Publishing LLC

041820

This book is dedicated to all the healthcare workers, first responders, and essential workers who toiled tirelessly through the spring of 2020.
What a strange world we live in.
Here's to a tiny bit of escapism.

story between series - with Josephine and Paul from The Letter.)

LIGHTHOUSE POINT ~ THE SERIES
Wish Upon a Shell - Book One
Wedding on the Beach - Book Two
Love at the Lighthouse - Book Three
Cottage near the Point - Book Four
Return to the Island - Book Five
Bungalow by the Bay - Book Six

CHARMING INN ~ Return to Lighthouse Point
One Simple Wish - Book One
Two of a Kind - Book Two
Three Little Things - Book Three
Four Short Weeks - Book Four
Five Years or So - Book Five
Six Hours Away - Book Six

SWEET RIVER ~ THE SERIES
A Dream to Believe in - Book One
A Memory to Cherish - Book Two
A Song to Remember - Book Three
A Time to Forgive - Book Four
A Summer of Secrets - Book Five
A Moment in the Moonlight - Book Six

INDIGO BAY ~ A multi-author sweet romance series

Sweet Days by the Bay - Kay's Complete Collection of stories in the Indigo Bay series

Or buy them separately:

Sweet Sunrise - Book Three
Sweet Holiday Memories - A short holiday story
Sweet Starlight - Book Nine

Sign up for my newsletter at my website *kaycorrell.com* to make sure you don't miss any new releases or sales.

CHAPTER 1

Lillian Charm walked into The Nest, the private area of Charming Inn she shared with her niece, Sara.

Sara looked up from where she was tapping away at her computer. "Good morning."

"Morning." Lillian headed straight for the coffeepot and poured herself a cup. "You're up early and busy this morning."

"I need to finish up this presentation. I have a meeting with Delbert Hamilton regarding promotion for The Cabot Hotel."

"That's a wonderful opportunity for you to get your name known in the area."

"I hope he likes what I came up with."

"I'm sure he will. You always have clever ideas for your advertising campaigns."

"And you're not biased at all." Sara grinned as she stood and snapped down the cover of her laptop. "I should head out."

"Have a good day."

"I'm having dinner with Noah tonight, so I'll see you later this evening."

"That's fine. I'm working the dinner shift in the dining room tonight, anyway."

Sara gathered her things and left, and then the kitchen was suddenly empty and quiet. She'd so enjoyed having Sara back here living with her even though her niece made noise about moving back out on her own. Lil was in no hurry for that to happen, though she understood how Sara might want her privacy. Especially now that she was dating Noah. Though Lil tried to give them as much time alone as possible.

She reached for the paper sitting on the table. Might as well have a leisurely cup of coffee and do the crossword. She felt only *slightly* guilty delaying the start of her workday. Sara was always telling her to slow down some. She was just taking her advice.

Not that slowing down would really ever happen. Charming Inn was still packed with guests even though the "snowbird" season was officially over. She really should head to her office. She'd left a long list of to-dos for today. Thank goodness she'd hired Robin, one of Sara's best friends, to help with the running of the inn. The busier they got, the crazier things were at the inn, and she did like things to run smoothly.

She folded the paper when she finished the crossword, pleased she'd figured out the whole puzzle, and set her cup in the sink. Time to get to work. With one last look around, she slipped out of The Nest and down the long hallway to the inn.

As she entered the main area of the inn, Robin waved to her from the reception desk where she was talking to some guests. She crossed over and waited until Robin was finished.

"It's been busy this morning. I tentatively booked a wedding for September, and Jay wants to see you. Some problem with Magnolia House."

Lillian sighed. "This rehab has been nothing but one problem after the next." She'd really thought when George and Ida wanted to sell their house next to Charming Inn that it would be a nice addition to the inn. A large, rambling house that guests could rent for big family gatherings. She'd paid a pretty penny for the property, too.

"I'm not sure what the problem is this time." Robin shrugged.

"I'll go find Jay and see what's going on." She might have hired him to be the chef, but Jay was super helpful with everything at Charming Inn.

More problems at Magnolia House had not been on her already too long to-do list.

GARY JONES ROLLED over in bed and looked at the bedside clock in shock. How in the world had he ever slept this late? He never slept in. He was always at work before dawn and came home late at night. But on his first night at Charming Inn, he'd slept a good ten hours.

Ten.

He couldn't remember doing that since he'd been a teenager, if then.

He guessed the stress of the last few months had finally caught up to him. He raked his fingers through his bed-ruffled hair and pulled himself up to lean against the stack of pillows.

Light streamed in through the doors to the balcony overlooking the gulf.

He'd chosen this place because it was about as far from home as possible. Far from everything he wanted to forget. Not to mention, his own son had asked him to leave for a while. Though his son—in his role of acting CEO— was probably right, and it was for the best. At least he'd raised his son to make smart decisions. Smarter decisions than *he*'d been making recently. That had been made crystal clear this year.

He dug the heels of his hands into his eyes to wipe away the sleep as well as a feeble attempt to erase his thoughts.

He stared outside at the brilliant blue sky sprinkled with fluffy white clouds. On a normal day, he'd have hours and hours of work behind him by now. And breakfast. He would have had breakfast by now. His stomach growled in answer to his thoughts.

Sliding his legs around, he set his feet on the worn wooden floor. It was warm and welcoming compared to the cold, stark tile floor of his apartment in Seattle. He glanced in the mirror and shook his head, barely recognizing himself. A couple days' growth of beard covered his face, and his hair was way past its usual four-weeks-on-the-dot limit. He ran his hand across his beard, debating shaving it off. But then decided to leave it. Why not break all the rules along with this ridiculous attempt at a vacation?

Vacation?

Why in the world should *he* be taking a vacation? What had he done that he deserved a break? Though, if he was honest with himself—which he'd sworn he would do from now on—it was more of an escape than a vacation.

The guilt slammed over him again, but he pushed it away. If he could only find a strong cup of coffee and wake up, maybe things would look better.

Maybe.

But he doubted it.

CHAPTER 2

L illian stood on the large wrap-around porch at Charming Inn. She frowned and shook her head. "Jay, you can't keep doing everything around here. I hired you to be our chef—the best one ever, by the way—but we need to hire some more help."

"I can take over for that lazy builder. Vince misses more days of work than he shows up."

"You can't take on that job, too. I appreciate the offer, but I'm going to have to find someone else."

"While you're at it, maybe find someone who really knows what he's doing." Jay shook his head. "Vince does everything halfway. I'm always going behind him and making sure he's doing things to spec."

"It's going to delay our opening of Magnolia House if we have to wait and find someone else." Lillian let out a long sigh, frustrated at all the delays.

"It might. But better the house and its new deck are made right and safe than the way Vince is doing it."

"I thought buying the house next door and rehabbing it was a smart business decision, but now I'm not sure."

"I still think it was a good idea. And Robin ran the numbers on it, didn't she? She thinks it's a smart purchase, too."

"I didn't think it would take this long to get it up and running. Anyway, you're right. I'm going to walk over to the work area and let him go."

"You could if he would have shown up today…" Jay rolled his eyes.

"Then I'll send him an email cancelling our contract with him. I'll list all the problems we've had and the delays. It was supposed to be finished by now. I'm glad we haven't booked anyone to stay there yet."

"The guy wouldn't know a deadline if it came up and smacked him in the face." Jay shook his head. "Wonder if Noah has the name of a good contractor?"

"He might. Let me deal with firing Vince, then I'll work on finding a new worker to finish up the rehab." She sighed. Just another task on her already long list.

GARY SAT around the corner from the lady and man having the discussion about rehabbing the house next door to the inn. A crazy thought crashed through his mind.

But no. It was too crazy.

Or was it?

It would at least keep him busy. If his hands were busy, maybe his mind would quiet down. Maybe he could feel like he was helping someone instead of hurting them...

He pushed up off the chair, still second-guessing himself, and rounded the corner. "Excuse me."

A woman—about his age, he'd guess, but he wouldn't bet his life on it—stood talking to a tall, thin, younger man with an apron tied about his waist.

"I'm sorry, did you need something?" The woman smiled at him.

"I… uh… I didn't mean to be… I mean I was just sitting around the corner and…" He shrugged. This wasn't coming out right. "Didn't mean to eavesdrop, but I heard you saying you were looking for a builder for finishing up rehab of the house and deck you're building."

"We are." The woman smiled again. A warm, welcoming smile that reached her honey-brown eyes. "I'm Lillian. Lillian Charm. I own the inn."

Ah, Lillian Charm. *Charming* Inn. He got it.

Lillian motioned toward the man. "And this is Jay, our chef and all-around fix-it man, but he's too busy for me to heap this job on him too even though he's a wizard with fixing things."

"And if I told you that I'm an experienced builder—a good one—and an accomplished carpenter. And if I told you I'm looking for a job while I'm here on the island, what would you say to that?"

The man—Jay—looked skeptical.

"How about we walk over to the house and I'll give you my opinion of the work that's been done. Look at the plans. Sounds like you know your way around a hammer and a drill." He looked at Jay.

The man stood there, still looking skeptical, in a black t-shirt stretched across his broad shoulders. The t-shirt said *First coffee and then... more coffee*. A hint of flour covered the hem of the shirt. At least they could agree on one thing —coffee.

"Jay, why don't you do that? Go over with Mr....?"

"Gary Jones." He held out his hand.

She took his hand, and he was surprised by her firm handshake. "I always listen to the universe when it drops an opportunity in my lap. I need a builder. You say you're one and need a job. I say it's serendipity."

Jay still didn't look convinced, but he untied his apron and handed it to Lillian. He cocked his head. "Let's go. I'll show you what's been done so far and the plans."

Gary didn't miss the look of doubt that crossed the young man's face as he led him off the porch and down a pathway. Guess he couldn't blame him. He knew better than most that a person should fully vet the people they hired.

CHAPTER 3

An hour later Lillian looked up from her desk as Jay walked into her office.

"I almost hate to say it because I was so skeptical, but this Gary guy knows his stuff. He also pointed out that the support posts Vince had ordered for the deck weren't large enough and he was certain they wouldn't be to code. He actually headed back to his room to read through the building code for Belle Island. Won't that be some light reading?"

"So you think we should hire him?"

"He said he doesn't have any recent references, and that bothers me, but he does seem experienced. Said he'd been out of the day-to-day construction business for quite a few years. Didn't say what he did now." Jay scowled.

"It's kind of crazy to just hire him on the spot, but I'd say… yes. At least give him a shot. What do we have to lose? I'll keep an eye on him and his work, too."

"See, serendipity. Just like I said." She smiled and stood. "I'll go up to his room and talk to him now."

She hurried through the inn and took the steps up to the suite Gary was staying in. It occurred to her that it was strange that someone who had rented the suite would be looking for work, but then, you never knew what was going on in other people's lives and she tried not to pry.

She knocked on the door and he promptly opened it. "Miss Charm."

"Lillian. Call me Lillian." She stepped into the room. "Jay says you know what you're talking about when it comes to rehabbing."

"I do. I worked quite a few years in construction."

"Well, the job is yours, if you want it."

"I do."

"Don't you want to know what I'm paying?"

"I'm sure it's fair." He shrugged.

"And you're able to stay here on the island until the job is completed?"

"I am." He nodded slowly. "That won't be a problem."

"I pay the going rate for this type of work and I'd like to comp your room, too."

"No need to do that."

"I insist."

He frowned. "How about I move into the house next door? It will make it easier to work on if I'm there, and you can have this suite for another guest."

She thought about it for a moment. It would be easier for him if he stayed where he was working, and the house really was beautiful, even if it needed a lot of work. The kitchen and bathrooms were functional at least. And she could always find paying guests for the suite.

She nodded. "Okay, that's a deal. And meals are on us, too. Here at the dining room."

"I won't say no to that. I'm not much of a cook."

"It's settled then?"

"It is. I'm just going to continue looking at these building codes. Had a few things I questioned over there. Then I'll move into the house and take an inventory of supplies there and what's needed. Then I'll be able to give you an estimate on how long until I can finish the job."

"Perfect. You can use the inn's van to pick up supplies, and we have an account at the hardware store in town."

"That will work."

"Sounds great." She held out her hand. "Pleasure doing business with you, Mr. Jones."

"Gary." His smile warmed his dark brown eyes as he shook her hand.

"Gary." She smiled back. She hoped she was doing the right thing with the sudden decision to hire a stranger. But sometimes the universe gave a person what they needed when they needed it. And she sure needed a builder right now.

GARY DROPPED his bag on the floor of the old house next door to the inn. The bones of the house were in good shape. It still had the original wood floors and woodwork, well worn now, but that just added to the charm of the house.

Sun streamed in the windows and made the dust dance in the light. He could see the potential in the house. He could also pick out the half-way done work of Lillian's previous builder. He frowned. He'd have to repair the ceiling where the prior worker had replaced a ceiling light. He'd check the wiring while he was at it. He'd noticed some torn screens, and the whole screen door on the front of the house needed replacing.

He should start a list. He looked around the kitchen searching for something to write on.

This day hadn't quite gone like he'd thought it would. He figured he'd just eat and mope around on this trip. Maybe do some beach walking.

Now look at him. He had a job to do. A purpose. He loved working with his hands and had missed the hands-on aspect of the actual building. His father had years ago insisted that he learn everything about the family business, and that included everything about day-to-day construction. He'd worked quite a few years on all types of construction jobs before moving on. And he missed those days. Really creating something with his hands.

This might be just what he needed.

At the very least it would keep him busy.

He almost felt guilty taking Lillian's money though. He certainly didn't need it. She could probably use it more than he. But he knew it would look strange if he said he'd do all this for free. And people might start asking questions. And *that's* the last thing he wanted.

He rummaged through the paperwork on a large table in the kitchen and found a yellow legal pad and pen. Perfect. He'd take a quick inventory and poke around. Then he'd go borrow that van and get supplies. Might as well get started right away.

A tiny bit of the gray fog that surrounded his days now started to split. Just a tiny bit, but he'd take whatever he could get.

CHAPTER 4

Noah paced back and forth in his cottage. He looked at his dog, Cooper. "What do you say? Do you think I have everything ready? Does it look nice?"

Cooper wagged his tail in answer.

"I'll take that as a yes." He looked around the room. Fresh flowers adorned the table, and he'd stretched his cooking skills to the best of his ability and made a fancy chicken dish for dinner. With any luck, it tasted as good as it smelled. He'd made veggies and a salad and picked up a couple of slices of fresh peach pie from Julie at The Sweet Shoppe. Julie was great at baking. He wasn't even going to attempt baking a pie.

"Shoot, the candles." He hurried over to a

cabinet and rooted around until he found two matching candles. That was a feat in and of itself. He usually only used candles if the electricity went out and then didn't care at all if they matched. He finally found two candlestick holders and placed them on the table. Then moved them around a little bit and messed with the flowers in the vase.

He stood back and surveyed his handiwork. Then moved the candles once more.

His glance darted around the room. Did it look okay? Would Sara wonder why he'd done things up so fancy tonight? He hoped not.

Because he wanted to surprise her.

He wanted the night to be perfect.

"Hey, you." Sara stood in the screened doorway.

"Come in." He crossed over to her, and she stood on tiptoe and kissed his cheek.

She looked around the room. "Wow, this is nice. Flowers and candles. And it smells delicious. What's the occasion?"

"No occasion. I just wanted to…" He searched for words. "Um, let you know how special you are to me and how glad I am we found each other again."

She smiled at him. That warm, endearing

smile of hers. The one that made the world fade away and he'd swear it was just the two of them.

She bent down to pet Cooper.

Okay, just the *three* of them.

"How about we have a glass of wine while dinner finishes?"

She nodded. He poured their drinks and led her to the couch. He almost knocked over his glass setting it on the coffee table.

"You okay?"

"Just a clumsy day, I guess." He'd better pull himself together. Dumping wine all over her would not be part of his well thought out plans. And he'd been planning this night for weeks.

"So I met with Delbert today. He likes my plans for the promotion of The Cabot Hotel." She stretched out her long, tanned legs.

"Of course he did. Your ideas are always brilliant."

She laughed. "You and Aunt Lil could become the public relations firm for my company."

"Does a PR firm need another PR firm for themselves?" He grinned.

The timer in the kitchen went off and he rose. "Stay and sip your wine. I'll go dish up the meal."

He hurried to the kitchen and served up dinner, trying his best to make it look presentable. He plated their food instead of his usual routine of just putting the cooking pots on the table. After finding the matches, he lit the candles. "Okay, it's ready."

Sara came into the kitchen. "It looks wonderful."

He held out a chair for her and she slipped into her seat. He wondered how he was going to eat and push the food past the lump in his throat.

Thankfully Sara chatted on about the details of her meeting with Delbert and all about Cabot Hotel, so he didn't have to do much to keep up his side of the conversation.

They finally got to dessert, and he heated the pie slices and put a scoop of vanilla ice cream on each piece. He glanced at his watch as he served up the dessert. He couldn't believe dinner had only taken thirty minutes. Felt like two hours. Maybe three. The night was crawling. He wanted to get dinner over and then—

"You okay?" Sara asked. "You seem kind of out of it tonight."

"I'm fine." He forced a smile and hoped it wasn't an awkward, nervous smile.

They finished their desserts—finally—and he cleared the table and poured them another glass of wine. He led her outside to the deck where the moon was streaming its light down and stars danced above them.

A perfect island night.

They settled on the glider and he turned to her. "Sara, these last few months have been... so... great. I mean, they've been *wonderful*. I'm so grateful I found you again."

She squeezed his hand. "I feel the same way. I'm happy we found each other again, too."

He cleared his throat. "I... I—"

"Noah?"

He rolled his eyes. This wasn't going quite according to plan. He took a deep breath to settle his nerves and slid down on one knee on the deck. "I love you, Sara Wren. I want nothing more than to spend the rest of my life with you." He took out the ring box that had been burning a hole in his pocket all evening and opened it. "Will you marry me?"

Sara's eyes flew open wide, then tears began to stream down her cheeks. She jumped up and tugged him to his feet and threw her arms around him. "Oh, yes, Noah McNeil. I'll marry you. I'd like nothing more than to spend the rest of my life with you, too."

He kissed her then, gently but thoroughly. He pulled away slightly and wiped the remains of her tears from her face. "We're going to have a wonderful life together."

"We are," she whispered back.

He was right. It was a perfect island night.

LIL SETTLED into her recliner and picked up her knitting. She'd just get a few more rows in on the cabled pillow she was making to brighten up the couch here at The Nest. She'd picked a shade of teal that went with the old worn woven teal throw that rested on the back on the couch.

No secret to anyone that teal was her favorite color. Always had been. Always would be.

She looked up as Sara entered the room. "Hello, dear. Did you have a nice evening?"

"Oh good, you're still up."

"I wasn't tired yet and thought I'd get in some knitting." She paused, looking at Sara's rosy cheeks and bright eyes. She set down her knitting. "Sara? What's up?"

"Oh, Aunt Lil…" Sara dropped to the floor beside the recliner and held out her hand. "Noah proposed."

"He did? That's wonderful." She let out a gasp of delight at the sight of the glittering ring and hugged her niece. "I'm so happy. For both of you." She tried to fight off tears of happiness but gave up and one or two rolled down her cheek. She wanted nothing more than her niece to find a love like she had with Noah. And find her happily-ever-after.

Sara jumped up and twirled around. "I know. I'm so happy. I love him so much."

"And he loves you. That's evident to anyone who sees the way he looks at you. Come show me the ring again."

Sara came over and Lil looked at the sparkling diamond set in a simple setting. It was so Sara. "It's lovely."

"I know. It's perfect, isn't it? He knows me so well." Sara jumped back up.

"Did you make any plans? Talk about when you want the wedding?"

"No, not tonight. He said he hopes I don't want a really long engagement because he wants to be married to me as soon as we can make it happen."

"Perfect. We'll work out whatever you two decide."

Sara twirled around again and Lil couldn't help but grin. Sara stopped and sank onto the couch, her cheeks flushed. "I can't wait to tell Robin and Charlotte. I was going to call them, but then I decided it would be more fun to tell them in person. Luckily, I'm meeting them for dinner at Magic Cafe tomorrow."

"That will be fun to tell them in person."

"So don't tell anyone until I get a chance to talk to them, okay?"

"Okay, I won't spoil your surprise. You know how news spreads like hurricane winds on Belle Island." Lil smiled. Today had turned out to be a pretty perfect day all in all.

CHAPTER 5

The next morning Lil woke up early, smiling as soon as she remembered Sara's news of last night. A momentary flash of sadness swept through her. Her sister, Leah, would have loved to see Sara marry, and she was sure Sara would miss her mother's presence at her wedding. But Lil would be there for her as she always had been.

When Sara was ready to start her wedding plans, she had a surprise gift for her. She'd been planning the surprise for years. Ever since Leah had died, years ago, and Lil had taken on the horrible job of cleaning out her sister's home.

She hoped Sara would be pleased with the gift.

She sighed, slid out of bed, and walked to the window, opening the blinds to let the light in. She'd slept later than usual after staying up late talking to Sara. Time to get a move on.

After getting dressed she went into the kitchen and found a note from Sara saying she'd left early and would see her later. Lil decided to grab coffee at the inn instead of brewing a pot and headed out, ready to start her day.

She entered the dining room and went straight to the sidebar that held the coffee urn. She poured herself a cup and turned to look at the morning crowd of customers enjoying their meals. Across the room, Gary Jones sat by himself, eating breakfast. She headed over to talk to him, stopping to greet a few customers at other tables on her way. She noticed he was clean shaven today and had an intent look of concentration as he jotted notes on a pad resting beside him.

Gary looked up when she got to his table. "Well, good morning, Lillian."

"Morning, Gary. Mind if I join you for a few moments?"

"Not at all." He motioned to the seat across from him.

She slipped into the chair. "Can we talk business while you finish your meal?"

"Good timing. I just finished." He pushed his empty plate to one side.

"Did you get all the supplies you needed?"

"Most of them. I did have to order in a few things that weren't in stock. They should be here soon, though." He flashed an impish smile at her. "I really wanted to get started working when I first got up this morning, but seeing as it was five a.m. I thought I might wait until a bit later to make noise. I did get a good schedule figured out though. What needs to be done first. Things like that."

"I'm very thankful that you heard Jay and I talking and offered to take over the job."

"I guess eavesdropping pays off sometimes." He chuckled. "At least in this case, it sure did. For both of us."

"It did."

He looked at her for a long moment. "You look particularly happy this morning."

"I… I am. Got some good news last night. I just can't…" She shrugged. "I'm sworn to secrecy until after this evening."

"I guess I'll have to wait until after this evening to see what you're so pleased about."

"I'm about to burst, but a promise is a promise."

"That it is." He nodded then pushed back from the table. "And now I should head back to Magnolia House and get to work."

Lillian stood. "I should get to work, too. Let me know if there's anything you need."

"I will." He turned and walked out of the dining room in long, confident strides.

She had a good feeling about him, like she'd made the right decision. And she almost always trusted her instincts about a person, and her instincts were telling her he was one of the good guys.

She sincerely hoped her instincts were right this time.

NOAH HAD BEEN fine with not telling anyone about the engagement until today, because his niece, Zoe, was coming to town. He couldn't wait to tell her the news in person. And he was certain that as soon as Sara had a chance to tell Charlotte and Robin, the news would spread through the island and everyone would know.

Zoe walked into his office at the community center and he jumped up to hug her. "You're early. I thought we were meeting at home at six?"

"I got off work early and decided to head on down here and avoid the traffic." She hugged him tightly. "I haven't been here in a while and I'm really looking forward to spending the weekend."

"I'm happy to see you. I miss you now that you're up in Orlando."

"Miss you, too." Zoe's eyes sparkled. "But I'm here now and we're going to fill the weekend with fun."

"Sounds good to me." He walked back around the desk and closed his laptop. Time enough to finish his work after Zoe left. "Let's head home."

They got home and Zoe walked into the kitchen, opened the fridge, and turned to him. "Want a beer?"

"I do."

She snagged them a couple of beers and leaned against the counter. "Yum, steak."

"Come on outside while I get the grill started."

They headed outside and he lit the grill,

then turned to Zoe, suddenly nervous about telling her the news.

They sat down and Zoe took a long look at him. "So… what aren't you telling me?"

"What? What do you mean?"

"You have that look on your face. Like you're trying to decide how to tell me something."

He laughed. "You know me so well."

"I do. So…"

"So, I asked Sara to marry me." He grinned sheepishly. "And she said yes."

"You did? That's wonderful." Zoe jumped up and hugged him. "I'm so happy. For both of you."

"I'm kind of happy for me, too."

"Tell me everything."

"Not much to tell. I invited her over for dinner."

"And you were a nervous wreck, I bet." She grinned as she sat back down.

"I was."

"Oh, I can't wait to see her ring. Did she love it?"

"I think so."

"So when do I get to see her?"

"She's out with Charlotte and Robin tonight

to tell them the news. We'll catch up with her tomorrow."

"Perfect." Zoe sighed. "I really am happy for you."

"Thanks, Zoe." He was so glad that Zoe liked Sara and Sara liked Zoe. It made everything just that much more perfect. And right now, he felt like his life was perfect.

Or it would be as soon as he married Sara.

ALL DAY long Sara had to keep from picking up the phone and calling Robin and Charlotte. But she really wanted to see their faces when she told them the news, so she resisted the urge. She resisted again and again.

When it was finally dinnertime, she walked into Magic Cafe about five minutes later than they'd planned to meet. She couldn't help it— she wanted to make sure they were both there, make a grand entrance, and show off her ring and tell her news.

Tally, the owner, hugged her when she entered. "There you are. Good to see you, Sara. How's Lil doing?"

She twisted her ring around on her finger so

Tally didn't see it. Not yet. Robin and Charlotte had to be the next people she told. "She's great. Recovered so well from her accident. You'd never even know it happened except for a very slight limp."

"It's hard to keep Lil down." Tally smiled. "Your friends are over there at a table by the sand. Perfect for watching the sunset. I'll bring a drink over for you. What would you like?"

"Do you have a bottle of champagne?"

Tally smiled. "A special night?"

"Just some good news."

"I'll bring a bottle right over."

She hurried over to the table, twisting her ring back in place. Robin looked up and her forehead wrinkled. "What's up? One, you're never late. Ever. And two… what's with that look on your face?"

She threw out her hand, flashing her ring. "Noah asked me to marry him."

"Oh, Sara. That's great." Charlotte jumped up and hugged her tight.

Robin came around the table and joined in the hug. "This is great news. I'm happy for you."

"I kind of want to pinch myself. I'm getting married. I'll be Noah's wife."

"Come, sit down. Tell us everything." Charlotte tugged her hand and led her to the seat beside her.

"The ring is gorgeous," Robin said as she sat down across from them.

"It's perfect for you," Charlotte agreed.

"I love it." She looked down at it again, not quite used to having it there on her finger. She was engaged. To Noah. After all these years.

"So, when did he propose?" Robin asked.

"Last night after dinner. He cooked this delicious meal. Had flowers and candles on the table. And he was acting a bit... strange. I should have known something was up, but I didn't."

"And?" Charlotte urged her on.

"And then we went outside in the moonlight and he got on one knee and asked me to marry him. It was so romantic. I'll remember that night forever." She let out a long sigh.

"The first one of us to marry." Robin smiled. "I'm really happy for you."

"And I can't wait to help plan the wedding," Charlotte added.

She laughed. "I'm not certain when the wedding will be, but I'm sure I'll take all the help with the planning that I can get. I only know that I want to get married at the inn."

"But of course." Robin nodded. "There's no other place as perfect."

Tally came over with the champagne in an ice bucket. "Here you go."

"Tally, I can tell you the good news now. Noah asked me to marry him." Sara showed Tally her ring.

"Ah, that is good news. Noah is a fine young man. I'm sure both of you will be very happy. And since it's such good news, the champagne is on the house. You three enjoy yourselves."

"Thanks, Tally."

As Tally left, Sara turned to her friends. "And you'll both be bridesmaids, right? No maid of honor, just fifty-fifty equal bridesmaids?"

"Of course." Robin nodded.

"I'd love to." A big smile spread across Charlotte's face. "This is going to be spectacular."

Robin poured each of them a glass of the champagne, then raised hers. "To Sara and Noah and a long happy life together."

The three friends clinked glasses and Sara couldn't imagine better friends to share her news and excitement with. She couldn't wait to plan her wedding with them...

... because she was engaged.

To Noah.

Happiness and a sense of rightness flowed through her. She was one lucky woman, and she'd never take it for granted.

CHAPTER 6

Gary sat out on the beach, watching the sunset. He trailed his fingers through the sand, writing random words and then smoothing them away.

When was the last time he'd just sat and watched a sunset? Or sunrise? Or anything for that matter? His life was always go, go, go. He rarely stopped to actually enjoy the moment.

And where had that got him?

Things were going to change, though. He was going to slow down. Look at the little details. Trust his instincts. *Listen* to them.

He was going to enjoy… well, enjoy the little moments.

Though brief thoughts taunted the edges of his mind. Why did *he* get to enjoy little moments? But as he'd carefully trained himself over the last months, he pushed those thoughts aside as best he could.

He looked out over the gulf and watched as a pair of pelicans swooped in unison along the coastline and then flew off into the distance.

He heard footsteps in the sand and looked up. An immediate smile crept across his face. "Lillian."

"I thought that was you." She smiled down at him.

"Join me." He patted the sand, welcoming her company.

She dropped beside him. "I decided to come out to catch the sunset."

"My plan exactly."

"With those big cloud pillars, I think it's going to be a spectacular display."

"So, can you tell me your big news yet?"

She turned to him, a wide smile on her face. "Yes, I can. My niece, Sara, got engaged. She swore me to secrecy until she had time to tell her best friends. I'm so happy for her. She's marrying a wonderful man."

"That is good news."

"She's like a daughter to me. I raised her

since she was a young girl. My sister... Leah. My sister and her husband..."

He heard the catch in her breath and the pain entering her words.

"They were killed in an accident. Sara moved here to live with me."

"I'm sorry." He gently covered her hand resting in the sand between them and she gave him a small, sad smile. "That must have been so hard on both of you."

"It was, but I don't regret a moment of it. I love the girl as if she were my own. It is sad, though, to think that my sister never got to see Sara grow up nor will she see her get married." Lillian took a deep breath. "Anyway, happy times around here, now. We're going to be planning a wedding. I couldn't be more pleased. I think Noah is the perfect match for Sara. I can't imagine how hard it would be if someone you love was marrying someone you thought was all wrong for them."

Gary frowned. He hadn't liked any of the long list of women his son had dated, though none of them had been serious relationships. He wondered if Mason would ever settle down. Not that he'd been a strong role model of good relationships himself. He and Mason's mother had split when Mason was just a young boy. Irreconcilable differences. Which, as far as he could tell, just meant neither of them wanted to put in the time to really work on the marriage or put that much effort into it. He'd married Jocelyn because it had seemed like the right time to settle down. To prove he was a responsible family man to the board of directors. Then they'd both been busy with their own careers and it had all fallen apart.

Just another regret in his life full of regrets.

"Do you have children?" Lillian's words broke through his thoughts.

"I do. A son. Mason."

"Where is he?"

"He… ah… he lives on the west coast. He's CEO of his own company now." He purposely kept the exact city vague.

"You must be so proud of him."

"I am." And he was. Mason had stepped up when it was needed and helped try to preserve what could be salvaged of the company.

"Is he married?"

"No, a confirmed bachelor."

Silence fell between them as the sky deepened into brilliant shades of pink, tinged with purple. But it was a comfortable silence as they sat and watched the beautiful theater that nature provided them.

Lillian finally broke the silence. "I should probably head back inside. Busy day tomorrow."

"I should, too." He rose to his feet, brushing the sand from his hands before offering one to Lillian.

She took his hand, and he helped her to her feet. She stumbled a bit as she rose.

"You okay?"

She frowned. "I am. I'm still recovering a bit from a little injury. I get a little stiff sometimes when I sit."

"Let me walk you back."

"That's not necessary."

"I'd feel better if you'd say yes."

She laughed. "If it'd make you feel better."

They headed across the beach and she led him to the side of the inn. "This is me. Sara and I call it The Nest. Our little private area of the inn."

"Well, good night then."

"Good night, Gary. Thanks for sharing the sunset with me. It was nice… peaceful."

"It was."

She slipped inside and he turned to head

back to Magnolia House. It *had* been peaceful. One of the few peaceful moments he'd had in months. Or longer.

Whether it was the beauty of the sunset or Lillian's company, it had been a magical evening.

Magical?

Since when did he think in terms like that?

ROBIN DUCKED into the kitchen at the inn and was pleased to find that Jay was still there. "Don't you ever go home?"

He turned and grinned at her. "I could say the same thing. What are you doing here so late? I thought you had dinner with Charlotte and Sara tonight."

"We did. And Sara had the best news." She paused and stared at Jay. "You don't look surprised or even look like you're waiting for me to tell you the big news."

"Sure I am. What is it?"

She slapped his arm. "You knew already, didn't you?"

"Knew what?" His face was a mask of exaggerated innocence.

"About Noah and Sara getting engaged."

"They did? That's great."

"Jay…"

"Okay, okay. I knew. Noah talked to me about it. He was a nervous wreck trying to plan the perfect evening to ask her. But then when you didn't say anything earlier today, I figured he'd lost his nerve or something went wrong last night. I was going to call him after I got home tonight and check."

"Sara wanted to tell us in person and we already had dinner plans tonight."

"I'm happy for both of them. They seem to fit well, don't they? Haven't seen Noah this happy since Zoe moved away."

"They do. I hope Zoe will be happy for them."

"I'm sure she will. Anything that makes her uncle happy makes Zoe happy." Jay reached above him, placing a stack of baking sheets high on a shelf.

His t-shirt stretched across his broad chest and she noticed a handprint of flour on the front of it. She looked away before he turned around and caught her staring at him.

"So I guess you three women will be big into wedding plans now."

Robin slid onto a counter stool next to Jay. "I'm sure we will. Once they set a date. Sara's total plan so far is that she knows she wants to have it at the inn."

"Of course." Jay nodded as he looked around the kitchen and folded the towel he was holding. "I'm finished up here. Can I walk you home?"

"Sure." She slid off the stool. She didn't even admit to herself that she'd grown to like their walks home together a few times a week. Jay insisted it was just because her bungalow that she shared with Charlotte was on the way to his cottage. Whatever it was, she enjoyed his company and found herself checking in on him at the end of the evenings.

They walked out into the night and headed down the sidewalk, walking in unison.

Yes, Jay was a good friend to have.

CHAPTER 7

G ary sat out on the old deck with his morning coffee. He needed to tear down the deck now that he had the new supplies. He was hoping to use some of the original boards when he remade it with stronger supports. But for now, he'd enjoy it as is.

He turned to a sound and saw a scraggly dog climb the stairs and stare at him. "Well, hello there. Where did you come from?" The dog stared at him with soulful eyes. He... or she... was overly thin and had no collar on. He held out his hand toward the dog, waiting to see if he—definitely a he—would come toward him. The dog just sat where he was.

"How about I find you something to eat?" He slowly rose and went inside, leaving the door open and talking to the dog as he searched for something to feed him. He hadn't gotten much in the way of food for himself... except for his coffee, of course. He saw nothing suitable for feeding the animal but did have a few bites of a sandwich left. That would have to work. He grabbed a bowl and filled it with water. At least he could give the pup a drink.

He went back outside and held out the partial sandwich toward the dog. When the dog wouldn't come to him, he set the sandwich down on the deck and the bowl of water beside it, then he backed away.

The dog crept forward, wolfed down the sandwich, and lapped up the water. "That's a good boy." When the dog backed away, he picked up the water bowl to fill it again. "I'll be right back."

He went inside and filled the bowl. When he came back outside the dog was gone. He looked up and down the beach but saw no sign of him.

He frowned. His next trip to town he'd pick up a small bag of dog food in case the pup came back. He must be a stray to be that thin. He'd do his best to fatten him up... if the pup would come back.

LILLIAN GOT UP EARLY and sat sipping coffee at the breakfast table, waiting for Sara to get up. She pretended she was doing the crossword puzzle, but she wasn't really concentrating. A flitter of excitement rushed through her. She'd waited a long time to tell Sara about the surprise she had for her. When Sara finally came into the kitchen, Lil pressed a cup of coffee into her hands. "Here you go."

"Thanks." Sara sank onto a chair.

Lillian sat back down. "So, did you have a good night with the girls?"

"I did. They're so excited for me. We're going to start planning the wedding. I need to sit down with Noah and pick a date. I want to have the wedding here at the inn if that's okay."

"Okay? It's wonderful. I can't imagine having it anywhere else." Her heart swelled with pleasure and joy. Sara's wedding here at Charming Inn. It didn't get more special than that.

"I'm a bit boggled by all the plans and decisions. How do people do this? So many things. A dress, invitations, food, flowers…"

Now seemed like the perfect time to show

Sara the surprise. "So… I have a surprise for you."

"You do? What?"

"Come upstairs to the attic with me."

"Okay." Sara, eyes curious, stood, and they climbed the stairs to the attic.

The dim light didn't do much to illuminate the space, so Lillian drew back the curtains. Light streamed in the window. "That's better." She walked over to the corner and pushed some boxes out of the way. "Here it is."

She brought the large box back to the pool of light dancing by the window. "I saved this for you."

Sara looked at the box and frowned. "What is it?"

"Open it."

Sara took off the lid and stared into the box.

"It's your mother's wedding dress."

"Oh, Aunt Lil." Sara gently lifted the dress from the box, folding away the tissue paper, carefully unwrapping it. She rose and held it before her, tears slowly rolling down her cheeks.

"I'm not sure what shape it's in. But I thought, even if you got it remade, you'd like to have the lace from it, at the very least. Your mother looked so lovely in this dress. It has the most beautiful lace." The memory of Leah's wedding poked at her heart, but she refused to let it dim the joy of Sara's wedding.

"It does." Sara lifted the fabric to the light and turned to her. "This is the most wonderful gift you could ever have given me. I'll feel... well, I'll feel like my mother is with me on my wedding day."

"She will be, Sara. She will be."

"This is so special." Sara hugged the dress close.

"Dorothy was talking at the Yarn Society the other day about a seamstress who was wonderful. She remakes old vintage clothing and is very talented. I could get her name and we could go talk to her. See what she could do for you. Even if you don't like the style, it could be made into something you do like."

"That would be wonderful." Sara walked over and pressed a kiss against her cheek. "Thank you so much. This will make my wedding even more special."

Lillian hugged her close. "You're welcome." She hoped this would lessen the pain of not having Leah here for the wedding, for Sara and for her.

CHAPTER 8

G ary stared at a loose board on the shiplap that lined the sunny front room at Magnolia House. The silly board had bothered him from the first day he'd seen the house. One board stuck out just a bit. He was probably too much of a perfectionist for his own good.

Though, he should have been more of a perfectionist with his company... He'd been so busy the last year, he'd pushed aside his hands-on approach to every detail of running the company because he'd thought he had it covered when he'd hired his college buddy, Brian. What a mistake that had been. From now on, it was back to overseeing all the details of anything he did.

He looked at the shiplap, trying to figure out the best way to fix it without tearing too much out. As he ran his hand along the board, his fingers snagged on a loose nail head. It was a different type of nail than had been used on the rest of the boards. That bugged him, too. He tugged on the nail, and to his surprise, the whole board swung wide revealing a hidden compartment behind the wall.

"Well, what do we have here?" He knew he was talking to himself, but the quiet of Magnolia House was starting to get to him. When he was back in his condo in Seattle—the few hours he was actually at his home and not at the office—he'd have the news on the TV droning in the background. Anything but total quiet.

He was trying to embrace the quietude of this guest house, but he hadn't quite gotten there yet. He turned at the sound of a knock at the front door. He hurried to answer it, leaving his newly discovered compartment behind him.

"Lillian. Perfect timing. Come see what I found." He was anxious to show off his discovery. Old houses often held many secrets.

She stepped inside. "What is it?"

He led her over to the open board. "Look, a secret compartment."

"Ooooh. That's interesting."

He reached his hand in, feeling around, and found something. He clasped his hand around it, pulled it out, and stared down at a worn leather journal with yellowing pages.

"I wonder if George and Ida left this here by mistake?"

"George and Ida?"

"They owned the house before I bought it. They'd lived here over forty years."

"Should I open it?"

"I guess so. Maybe we'd at least be able to tell whose it is."

He carefully opened the cover and saw the date. "I'm pretty sure this is from before George and Ida." He showed her the date of the first entry. January 1, 1898.

"Goodness, that's old. Is there a name in it?"

He leafed through the pages. "None that I can see."

"It feels kind of wrong to read it, but maybe if we do, we can figure out whose it is and give it back to their family."

He handed it to her. "Here, you can read it.

You'll know more about the island than I do and maybe you can figure out who wrote it?"

"I'm not sure. It was a long time ago. But maybe there'll be some kind of hint in it." She took the journal from him and held it close. "But I'll give George and Ida a call, just to make sure. Maybe they know something about it."

"Good idea."

He reached his hand in the compartment again, feeling along all the edges and corners. His hand closed over something and he pulled it out and opened his fist. A single piece of turquoise-colored sea glass rested in his palm.

"Oh, that's pretty."

He reached out and gave it to her, their fingers brushing as he dropped it onto her palm. "That's all I can find in there."

"A mystery. I wonder why someone put the sea glass in there? There's not a lot of sea glass to be found on the beaches around here. Nothing like on the east coast, especially further up north." She turned the glass over and over in her hand, examining it closely.

Or all the sea glass on Alki Beach near where he lived in Seattle, but he wasn't going to offer that information. The less people knew about him, the better. Maybe they could get to know him before they judged him by his one terrible and tragic mistake.

LILLIAN HURRIED into the community center for the Yarn Society meeting that afternoon. She was just brimming with news and couldn't wait to tell everyone. Dorothy and Ruby waved to her as she entered, and she went to grab a chair beside them.

"Where's Mary?" she asked as she sat down and tugged out her knitting project.

"Adam was taking her to the doctor. Just a regular checkup," Dorothy said. "Though she is getting more forgetful and I know he's worried about her. He said that maybe the doctor could adjust her meds."

"It must be so hard on Adam seeing his mother suffer through Alzheimer's." Ruby shook her head. "Horrible disease. I hope they can find a cure, and sooner rather than later."

Dorothy nodded. "At least Mary can still do things at Belle Island Inn like seat people in the dining room and help in the kitchen. She enjoys that. I imagine it helps her feel needed. Anyway, I'm there to help her too, in any way I can."

"You're a good friend, Dorothy." Lillian picked up her knitting, concentrating on figuring out where she'd stopped on her project the other night.

"Ah, she'd do the same for me," Dorothy brushed off the compliment. "So, anyone have any good news?" She looked directly at Lillian over the top of her reading glasses.

Lil laughed. "So, I see that the news of Sara's engagement has already spread."

"It has. I've heard it from at least three people today." Ruby laughed. "You must be so happy. Noah is a fine young man."

"I am pleased. And I had a surprise for her this morning. I saved my sister's wedding dress all these years. I gave it to Sara, and she's going to use it to have a dress made for her own wedding."

"Oh, that's such a fabulous idea," Ruby's eyes lit up.

Lil turned to Dorothy. "So I want to get the name of that lady you said remade vintage clothes and did special sewing projects."

"Sure, her name is Kristen Fellows. She has business cards up at Bella's shop on Oak Street.

"She does really nice work. I've seen it. Her

stitching is excellent and she's very clever with her ideas." Ruby nodded.

"How do you know so much about her work?" Lillian asked.

"I saw some of her pieces at Bella's shop. I used to design and make my clothes in my younger days. Kind of a hobby. So I always love to see work like that." Ruby smiled. "Somewhere along the way of raising boys, my ambition to become a famous designer got pushed aside."

"Didn't know that about you," Lillian said. "I'll drop by Bella's after this and grab a card so we can contact her." She set down her knitting and rooted around in her bag. "I have other news." She pulled out the leather journal.

"What's that?" Ruby asked.

"We found it in a hidden compartment in the wall of Magnolia House. Gary, the man I hired to help with the rehab, found it."

"What happened to Vince? I thought he was doing the work for you?" Dorothy paused her knitting needles.

"Vince was... problematic. I let him go. Then this Gary was practically dropped in my lap. Jay says Gary's doing a good job, though he's only been at it a few days."

"That was lucky. Sometimes it's very difficult to find good help here on the island," Ruby said. "I'm lucky that David is so handy. He's fixed so many things at the house for me."

"Always pays to marry a handy guy." Dorothy grinned and turned back to Lillian. "So, what's in the journal?"

"I haven't really read much yet. It's from 1898, can you believe that? But I haven't seen any names yet. I'll look more closely at it tonight. Maybe I'll find some clues to who wrote it."

"Can I see it?" Dorothy reached for the journal and leafed through it. "Hey, here's a few sentences about meeting friends at the beach for the Sandcastle Festival. I guess the island has always been into their festivals." Dorothy grinned.

"I guess we have." Lillian smiled. "And we have the Palm Festival coming up."

"Between working on the festival and planning his wedding, Noah's going to be a busy man," Dorothy said.

"That he is," Lillian agreed as she settled her knitting needles into a steady rhythm.

CHAPTER 9

Gary browsed through the aisles of the hardware store looking for the few items on his list. Seemed like there was always just one more thing he needed. He paused and squinted to read the small printing on a package of decking screws. Why did companies insist on such small printing? He should have grabbed his reading glasses and stuffed them in his pocket, but usually, he tried to ignore that fact he needed them.

"Garrett? Garrett Jones? Is that you?"

He whirled around at the unexpected sound of his given name, his heart pounding. "Uh…" He looked at the man standing before him.

"Reed Newman, remember me? We worked on the fundraiser for the Seattle Arts Center."

Yes, he remembered him. Reed Newman, fellow Seattleite. What were the chances? "Reed, good to see you." But it really wasn't. Not at all. Though he did have manners and extended his hand to the man.

"What are you doing here?" Reed shook his hand.

"Just a bit of… vacation. What are you doing here?"

"I live here now. Well, most of the time. Still commute back and forth to Seattle." Reed looked at him closely. "So, how are you doing?"

Gary recognized that look. One of sympathy and a bit of judgment, though he might be imagining that part. He knew he was overly sensitive after everything that had happened.

He never was sure how to answer that question so he went with, "As well as can be expected."

Reed nodded. "You going to be here long?"

"For a bit. I'm helping out Lillian Charm at Charming Inn. Rehabbing a house she bought next door to her inn that she's going to use as a guest house."

Did Reed look surprised at that? That he'd

be building something? Or was he once again being overly sensitive?

"That sounds like that will keep you busy."

"Yes, it should." He paused and looked at Reed. "And… people here know me simply as Gary Jones. I'd kind of like to keep it that way if you don't mind."

"I don't mind a bit. Gary Jones it is." Reed shook his hand again. "Maybe I'll see you around the island."

Gary nodded. Reed turned and left the store. As Gary watched him leave, a sinking feeling pressed on in his chest. It was hard to keep his identity a secret. Sooner or later he was afraid it would get out.

And then he'd see those judgmental looks again. The ones he'd been trying to hide from… though, he really did deserve them all. He even kind of looked at himself that way.

AFTER FINISHING UP A LATE DINNER, Sara, Noah, and Zoe sat at Magic Cafe. Zoe had been nonstop with questions about the wedding, but Sara didn't mind.

"So, you're going to have your mother's

dress made into a dress for your wedding? That is so cool," Zoe said as she reached for her wineglass. "I wish... well, that's not possible. We don't have my mom's wedding dress. Not that I'm even dating anyone seriously."

"I'm sorry, kiddo. I didn't even think to save it." Noah looked forlorn.

"Uncle Noah, don't apologize. I still don't know how you jumped in and took care of me and raised me." She grinned at him. "You did a great job if I do say so myself."

"I admit I didn't know what to pitch and what to save back then. I saved photo albums and a few things from your parents."

Once again Sara thought about how parallel Zoe's and her own life had been. She'd been raised by her aunt when her parents died, and Zoe by Noah when his sister had died.

"Zoe, I wanted to ask you something." She looked at Zoe. "Would you like to be one of my bridesmaids?"

"She can't," Noah interrupted.

"Why not?" Zoe looked at him with raised eyebrows.

"Because I want you to be my best man. Or best woman. Or best person." Noah's face had a pleading look.

Zoe laughed. "I can't say no to you, Uncle Noah. Of course, I'll be your best whatever." She turned to Sara. "Sorry."

"No, that's great. I just wanted to be sure you were included in the wedding party." That really was perfect for Zoe to be Noah's best person. She couldn't be happier for both of them. So far the wedding plans were coming along nicely.

She only hoped the rest of the planning went just as smoothly.

Zoe stood. "If you two don't mind, I'm off to meet Lisa at The Lucky Duck. Haven't seen her in a while. I'll probably be late. Don't wait up for me." Zoe turned to Sara. "Sometimes he forgets I'm a grown woman and does silly things like wait up to make sure I get home okay when I'm here visiting."

"I don't think that's silly," Noah said defensively.

Zoe rolled her eyes, turned away, and said back over her shoulder, "I'll see you later. Hopefully it will be *morning*, not late tonight."

Sara smiled at the exchange between Zoe and Noah and her heart swelled a bit with more love for this man and his concern for his niece. They sat and finished their wine. He drove her home and walked her up the steps to The Nest. He wrapped his arms around her and drew her close. "I can't wait to marry you."

She rested her head against his chest, soaking in his warmth. "I can't wait to marry you, either. You make me so happy."

He pulled her closer. "And that's my job. To make sure I make you happy. Always and forever."

LILLIAN SETTLED in bed that night with the leather journal. She'd left a message with George and Ida but hadn't heard back from them. Though, the journal had been written decades and decades before George and Ida had bought the house. She doubted if they even knew of its existence because why would they have put it back in the wall? Good thing Gary had such an eagle eye and spied the out-of-place board.

She ran her hand over the smooth leather cover and carefully opened it to the first page. The first few pages gave her no hints about the writer, though the handwriting looked like it was from a female with all the extra pretty swirls.

But she wasn't positive. She randomly turned to a later section in the journal and read the entry.

July 10, 1898

Clara, Jane, and I went to the Sandcastle Festival. Johnny was there, but I didn't get a chance to talk to him. Papa was keeping a close eye on me. But Clara, Jane and I did win the sandcastle contest. That was fun. The prize was ten whole dollars to the General Merchandise Store. We're going to all three go shopping together this week. I can't wait. I want to get a new dress for the dance next weekend.

That didn't help with the writer's name, but it did give her three other names. Two friends and Johnny. Who was this mysterious Johnny? Someone the writer didn't think Papa would approve of? More questions.

She closed the journal and set it on the night table. Maybe some other entries would give her more clues or maybe George and Ida might have some information. She picked up the piece of turquoise sea glass and turned it over and over in her palm as if that would give her some answers.

Nothing.

She set it on top of the journal. Maybe she'd find answers later, but now, she needed to rest. Tomorrow was a busy day, but then when was a day not busy? But that was okay with her.

CHAPTER 10

L illian seated a group of four customers at a table by the window the next evening, then looked up and saw Sara and Noah coming into the dining room, arm in arm. She smiled just seeing their happy faces. She wanted nothing more than she wanted her niece's happiness. She waved to them and they met her halfway. "So, did you come for dinner?"

"We did. Can you join us?" Sara asked. "Please?"

Lillian looked around at the room. "Let me just talk to the hostess. Let her know she can come get me if she needs me." She returned and the three of them sat a table in the corner.

Sara shifted in her chair and played with the spoon beside her plate. Something was up with her niece, she was sure of it. She waited patiently for Sara to tell her.

Sara finally stopped fidgeting and looked directly at her. "So, Noah and I have set a date, we think."

"You have? That's great news." Lillian ran through when she thought they'd picked. Maybe a Christmas wedding? Sara loved Christmas. That was only like eight months away, though. They could plan a wedding in eight months, couldn't they?

Sara continued, "I checked on the inn's calendar and the date is available for a wedding on the day we want. I tentatively added it to the schedule. We want to get married in—if you think it's possible—in four weeks." Sara looked at Lil, her expression worried and excited at the same time.

Lil sat for a moment, glad she'd held back her gasp of surprise. Four short weeks. That wasn't much time. But if that's what Sara wanted, then that's what they'd do.

"I think that's wonderful. I'm sure we can make it happen." She wasn't *sure* though. Her mind bounced from thought to thought on all that would have to be done.

Sara grinned, and Noah leaned over and

kissed her cheek. "See, I told you we could make this work and Lil would be fine with it." He squeezed her hand and turned to Lillian. "My fault. Now that I've asked her to marry me, I just don't want to wait."

"I'm going to tell Charlotte and Robin later tonight. We'll start making lists. Robin is great with lists." Sara laughed.

"I got the name of the seamstress from Dorothy. I guess we'll have to see if she can fit us in her schedule to have the dress in four weeks, though."

Sara frowned. "I really want the dress for the wedding. I have my heart set on it."

"We'll try to make it happen then." Lillian nodded. If it was important to Sara, it was important to her. One way or another, they'd make it work.

Sara grabbed a notebook from her purse. "Okay, I actually *have* started a list. See?" She held up a page with writing on every line. "I'm going to put a star by contact the seamstress, though. I'll do that first thing tomorrow."

"Good idea." Lillian nodded.

They came up with more items for her list until their dinners came and Sara put down the notebook.

Sara turned to Lillian. "Tell Noah about the journal you were telling me about this morning at breakfast."

Noah looked at her expectantly.

"Gary found this old journal. Gary—he's doing the rehab work now, I guess Sara told you?"

Noah nodded.

"Anyway, he found this old journal hidden in the wall. It's dated 1898. I started reading some of it last night, trying to find out who it belonged to. So far I don't know who's writing, but I did find a few names mentioned. I don't know if that will help me much. The journal said the writer and her two friends, Clara and Jane, won the sandcastle building contest at the Sandcastle Festival back then."

"Ah, so our many festivals come from a long tradition on the island?" Noah grinned.

"It appears they do."

Noah's forehead wrinkled. "You know, I did some research for an article I wrote for the town paper. I was researching the start of the community center. It's been in existence for years in one form or another. But I did find out the historical society has scans of a lot of the old newspapers. I think it was called The

Lighthouse Times back then, just like now. If I remember right, they had a society section in the paper. Things like relatives of the townspeople coming to visit. Or famous people coming to the island. Even things like the Ladies' Bridge Club being held at this person or that person's house. Or someone's kid going off to college. Just local news. You might try looking there."

"That's a fabulous idea. I'll do that as soon as I have time, though it looks like I'll be pretty busy with the wedding."

Talk turned back to the wedding with Sara grabbing her notebook and jotting notes as they sat and ate and made plans.

Lillian had to give Noah credit, though, he didn't look a bit overwhelmed by the growing list of to-dos and even offered to do many of them. Somehow, between Sara and Noah, and Charlotte and Robin, plus herself, they'd make this a magical wedding. She was sure of it.

Pretty sure.

It was still only four short weeks…

Robin stopped by the kitchen to make sure

everything was going well with dinner this evening. As manager of the inn, she needed to check on things like that. Or at least that was the excuse she was giving herself.

Jay sat by the computer in the corner of the kitchen. He turned to her when she entered. "Hey, you didn't tell me." He looked at her accusingly.

"Tell you what?"

"That Noah and Sara have picked a wedding date."

"They have?" Robin walked over to Jay and peered over his shoulder at the computer screen.

"Yes, I was looking at the calendar for next month to see what bigger events we have going to plan the food and order supplies..." He pointed at the screen. "See here? It says Sara and Noah's wedding. Four weeks away."

"I—no, she wouldn't do it that soon. We haven't planned anything."

"I don't know... that's what the calendar says. Noah didn't say a word to me, either."

Robin tugged out her cell phone to see if she'd missed any messages. Nope. She glanced at the time.

Jay laughed. "You're going off to find Sara, aren't you?"

"I am." She nodded vigorously. "Why wouldn't she have told Charlotte and me?"

"I don't know." He shrugged. "But Sara, Noah, and Lil ate dinner here tonight. Maybe they just decided?"

"Are they still here?"

"No, they left."

"I'm going to head to The Nest and see if I can find her." She tugged out her phone as she walked away and called Charlotte.

"Char, you know anything about Sara setting a date for the wedding?"

"No. She hasn't said anything to me."

"According to the calendar at the inn, she's picked one... and it's in four weeks."

"No." There was no missing the surprise in Charlotte's voice.

"I'm headed to The Nest right now to see what's going on. Maybe it got added to the wrong month?" Maybe that was it? A simple little mistake like that? One wrong click and it was put on the wrong date? Maybe the wrong *year?*

"I'm coming over, too. I'll be right there." Charlotte hung up.

Robin hurried off to The Nest.

SARA SAT with her aunt out on the deck of The Nest. Noah had gone home, but she'd been restless with all the excitement and Aunt Lil had suggested they have a glass of wine out on the deck. The stars twinkled above them and a light breeze blew in from the sea. She sat and let the evening soothe her.

They tried to talk about the inn or the weather or anything but the wedding so Sara could settle down. But eventually, all talk turned back to wedding plans. She guessed this was just the way it would be for the next few weeks.

"Sara, there you are."

Sara and Lillian turned at the sound of Robin's voice.

"Hey, Robin."

"Don't hey Robin me like you're not hiding the biggest secret ever. You picked a wedding date and didn't even tell Char and me?"

"How did you…" Sara shook her head and laughed. "It's on the inn's calendar already. You saw it, didn't you?"

"Actually Jay saw it and pointed it out to me. But it's on the calendar for four weeks from now."

"Yes, that's right. And I was going to call you and Charlotte later tonight and tell you." Sara sighed. "I should have talked to Jay, too. He'll be busy with food prep for the wedding."

"I need a glass." Robin disappeared into The Nest and returned with two glasses. "Char's headed over, too."

"Of course she is." Sara grinned. She'd expect nothing less from her friends than immediate questions and unwavering support.

"We have lots to plan if we have a wedding to pull off in four weeks." Robin poured herself a glass, then one for Charlotte, and sank into a chair beside them. "We can do it though. If this is what you want, we'll make it happen."

"We don't want a big wedding. Just close friends. Something simple."

Charlotte walked up the stairs to the deck. "Simple? I can do simple. I think. But I have all these great ideas. I've been thinking about them ever since you got engaged. Which was only a couple of days ago, by the way." Charlotte swooped up the fourth glass of wine, took a sip, and sat beside Robin.

"Char, I was going to call you later tonight."

"But we found out first. No secrets here on the island, that's for sure." Her friend leaned back in her chair and stretched out her long, tanned legs, kicking off her sandals. "We're going to be busy, aren't we?"

"We need to make a list. A master list." Robin jumped up. "Lil, do you have a pad of paper? And I need some light out here to write."

"There's a pad of paper in the drawer in the desk and a couple of battery-operated lanterns just inside the door. That should be enough to write by."

"Let me get my list, too." Sara got up to retrieve her notebook.

"Okay, let's write down everything that needs to be done, then we'll split it up." Robin sat with her pen poised over the pad of paper.

"I'll call about my wedding dress tomorrow," Sara said.

Robin scribbled a note.

"We can see if Julie at The Sweet Shoppe will make the wedding cake. She makes wonderful cakes," Lillian added.

"I can do the decorations. I was thinking mason jars with fairy lights in them scattered around on the deck of the inn. And we'll put flowers on the arbor. And bows on the back of the chairs. And—"

"The lights sound pretty, but nothing too

fancy, okay?" Sara interrupted Charlotte before she had the whole inn or maybe the whole island decorated for the wedding.

Charlotte sighed. "Okay. Simple. Like I said, I can do simple. Probably." She grinned. "This is going to be so fun."

"Noah and I will talk to Jay tomorrow about food. Aunt Lil, will you join us?"

"Of course." Lil nodded.

"I've already done some browsing online for invitations." Charlotte grinned again. "Couldn't help myself. But I did find some that are simple but classic, and I think you'll love them."

"We really just want small. A few friends."

"Good luck with that. You know how things go on the island… small events here have a way of growing." Robin jotted another note.

"Small. Promise me." Sara eyed her friends.

"Sure thing. Small."

But Sara didn't miss the doubtful look in Robin's eyes.

CHAPTER 11

The next morning Lillian and Sara sat at the kitchen table working on the wedding guest list. "And don't forget Tally." Lillian nodded toward the ever-growing guest list.

"I have her and Julie and Susan."

"I'd like to have a few friends from The Yarn Society if that's okay."

"Of course I want your friends here."

Lillian eyed the list. The growing list. "That's Ruby and David, of course. And Dorothy and Mary."

Sara sighed. "I know that Noah is going to have a pretty good-sized list, too. It's like he knows everyone in town. How am I going to have a simple wedding if it's getting so big?"

"Simple and big are not mutually exclusive.

We'll figure it out." She got up to pour them more coffee but paused when she heard a knock. "Let me get that."

She went to answer the door. "Ruby, hi. Come in."

"I was out walking with Mischief. Mind if he comes in, too?"

"Not at all." She bent down to pet the pup. "Sara and I were just sitting down in the kitchen, working on wedding plans. Come join us."

She poured Ruby some coffee and they sat down.

"I think I'll go try and call the seamstress." Sara got up. "I'll be back."

"What's all this?" Ruby pointed to the papers on the table.

"That's Sara's wedding guest list. She's decided to get married..." Lillian paused and shrugged. "In four weeks."

"That's not long, but I've heard it can be done in that short of time." Ruby smiled. "We did plan my wedding in just a month, and it turned out perfect."

"I'm sure we can make it happen. I just want it to be so special for Sara."

Ruby reached over and touched her hand. "It will be. I'm sure it will."

Sara came back into the kitchen and it was clear from her crestfallen look that the call hadn't gone well. She sank into her chair. "She can't do it. She has a project she's finishing up this week, then she's headed to visit her mother in Montana for three weeks. What am I going to do? I really want to wear Mom's dress. Or something made from it. Do you think I should postpone the wedding? Noah will be so disappointed."

"Sara... if I'm not intruding... could I see the dress?" Ruby asked.

Sara got up and retrieved the dress. Ruby looked it over carefully. "It's beautiful."

"It is. And... well... I want to wear it for my wedding. Maybe change out the style a bit. But —" Sara sighed. "I don't know what to do."

"I could help you with that," Ruby offered.

Sara's eyes lit up. "You could?"

"I used to design all my clothes when I was younger. I sewed constantly." Ruby looked at the dress again. "We could take off the long sleeves, or at least make them short, cap sleeves. And shorten the dress length a bit. Change the neckline. Here, give me a piece of that paper."

Lillian watched as Ruby sketched a dress on the paper. It was similar to Leah's dress, but a bit simpler and more suited for Florida's climate.

"I love that." Sara clapped her hands.

"I can do this for you." Ruby looked at them expectantly.

"Are you sure?" Lillian asked. "It looks like a big job."

"I'd love to do it."

"Then, yes. I'd love for you to fix the dress for me." Sara's eyes glistened with tears. "It will mean so much to me to wear my mother's dress."

"Then it's decided." Ruby nodded. "So, how about you bring the dress to my house later today? I'll take your measurements and I'll do a better drawing. Then I'll get started."

"Perfect." Sara let out a long sigh. "Now I hope everything else falls into place like this did." She rose. "I'm going to go call Noah. I'll see you this afternoon, Ruby. And again, thank you so much."

"You're welcome."

Sara walked away and Lillian turned to Ruby. "You're certainly a godsend for this dress. Wearing it means the world to Sara... and to me, too. It will make it seem like Leah is at the wedding in a way."

"I'm happy to do it." Ruby's eyes sparkled. "I'm actually excited about it. I've been meaning to get out my sewing machine again and try my hand at designing a few things. This will be a great start. I've missed doing this. When I was raising the boys, the most sewing I did was fixing rips and sewing on patches."

Lillian smiled. One thing on the list checked off. A million more things to do.

LILLIAN WALKED into the kitchen at the inn, humming under her breath. "Good morning, Jay."

"Morning, Lil. You're in a good mood considering the month you have ahead of you." Jay grinned.

"So, you heard about Sara's wedding." Lillian walked over to where Jay was cooking an order of eggs on the grill.

"I did."

"Sara and I would like to meet with you today and we'll discuss the food."

"Whenever you want." Jay nodded.

"And did you see Gary this morning? Did he come for breakfast? I want to check with him and see how things are going on Magnolia House."

"I don't think he did."

"Maybe I'll grab a couple of your cinnamon rolls and bring them over to him."

Jay nodded toward the tray of delicious-looking cinnamon rolls dripping with vanilla icing. The tantalizing aroma of yeast and cinnamon taunted her. Maybe she'd just take a few more of them and join Gary.

She boxed up the rolls and headed to Magnolia House, deciding to walk up the beach to it. When she got to the house, she was met with a surprise. Gary had dismantled the old deck, and a stack of the old boards rested on the sand. He had new posts placed in the corners of where the deck would be and other scattered support posts in place.

He looked up at her and smiled as she approached. The man did have a warm, friendly smile. His eyes lit up with his smiles, and faint wrinkles crinkled the corners of his eyes. "Good morning."

"Morning. You've been busy." She nodded at the missing deck and smiled. "And Jay said you didn't come over for breakfast, so I brought you some cinnamon rolls."

"I got busy early this morning and just didn't make time to eat."

"Got time to take a break now? They're still warm. Or they were when I left the kitchen."

"Sounds excellent. We'll have to go around to the side to get inside until I get this deck finished."

She followed him around the house and inside to the kitchen, noticing he'd replaced the old light fixture and the sink had a new faucet instead of the old banged-up one.

He washed his hands at the sink and popped open the box she handed him. "Will you join me?"

She laughed. "I was hoping you'd ask me. They smell so wonderful. Jay makes the best cinnamon rolls."

Gary grabbed some plates and a couple cups of coffee and they sat down at the table after he cleared some papers away.

"Oh, these are good." Gary nodded after he tried the delicious treat.

"Told you. Jay is one of the best hires I've ever made. Well, and Robin. It's wonderful to have Robin help me run the inn." And so far, she was pleased with hiring Gary, too. He'd done more in these few days than Vince had done in weeks on end. She was glad she'd fired Vince, though she'd heard rumors he was bad-mouthing her around town, but she mainly ignored the gossip.

"I'm sure hiring Robin does help. It must be a lot of work running the inn."

"It is, but I love it." She shrugged.

"I worked on the plumbing in the upstairs bathroom last night. Couldn't sleep and figured it wouldn't make noise for your neighbors like when I'm out hammering on something."

"Or tearing down the old deck?"

"Or that." He smiled. "I'm hoping to use a lot of the old wood. Save you some money. Plus, it has character. I should have it replaced in a few days."

"You're really going quick on all of this."

"Should have everything finished in a few weeks or so. Hope that timeline is okay with you."

"It's perfect. Maybe it will be finished in time for Sara's wedding. I'm sure we could use it for guests then. I'm trying to set some rooms aside at the inn for wedding guests, too. Though

Sara says she wants a small wedding. I'm not sure how small it actually will be."

A confused look crossed Gary's face. "I thought your niece just got engaged."

"She did. But now she and Noah have decided to get married in four weeks."

Gary's eyebrow raised. "That will make for a busy month, won't it?"

"It will. But I'm okay with that."

"I'll make sure to have Magnolia House done by then, so plan on having it available for guests."

"That would be wonderful." She smiled at him. "Oh, and I'll send Charlotte over to pick paint colors for the walls. She has such a good eye for that. George and Ida left some of these wonderful pieces of furniture, but we'll need more. I'll put Charlotte on that, too. She's helped with picking out paint and furniture for a couple remodels of the cottages."

"Sounds good. I'm a great painter, but not so great on picking out colors that work well together." He took another big bite of the cinnamon roll, then wiped his mouth, grinning. "Really good."

She smiled at his enthusiasm. Though, she'd

finished almost half of her own cinnamon roll already too. It *was* good.

"So, have you figured out who wrote the journal?"

"No, not yet. But Noah had a good idea to try the historical society. I have a few clues from the journal. I'll see what I can find." She'd hoped to have time to read more of it last night, but it had been late when Robin and Charlotte finally left. She'd try to make time tonight to read more, then find time to get to the historical society. You know, along with all the plans for the wedding.

But she felt confident now that she'd done the right thing in hiring Gary, so there was that.

Gary jumped up from the table suddenly. "Oh, hey there, pup."

She turned to where Gary was looking out the screen door. A scraggly looking dirty-brown and white-*ish* dog sat on the other side of the screen.

"I got you some food, bud." Gary went to a cabinet, poured some food in a bowl and filled another bowl with water. Lillian got up to open the screen door for him, and the dog backed away a safe distance, eyeing them.

"I'll just put this down for you and we'll go

back inside, okay, bud? Then why don't you eat this all up? You look like you could use a few good meals." He kept his tone low and soothing.

They went back inside and sat down. The dog slowly crept up to the food bowl, then scarfed down every bit of food before lapping at the water.

"Who's your friend?" Lillian nodded toward the screen door.

"Not sure. He showed up the other day. All I had was a left-over sandwich for him, so I bought some dog food in case he came back. He's all skin and bones, and kind of skittish. He came back last night, and I fed him some food. Talked a bit to him. I was hoping he'd come back today."

"He doesn't have a collar."

"No. If I can ever win him over, I'll get him a bath and take him to a vet to see if he's micro-chipped."

"I hope he keeps coming back and you can fatten him up, poor thing."

"I do, too."

This Gary was a kind man. He'd gone out of his way to pick up dog food on the off-chance the stray dog would come back. She smiled at him.

"What was that smile for?"

"Just—I'm just very glad to have you here and working on the house." She grinned. "And saving puppies."

He grinned back at her, his eyes twinkling, and took another bite of his cinnamon roll.

LILLIAN LEFT and headed back down the beach toward the inn. Gary stood next to the pile of decking boards, watching her walk away. She did have the tiniest limp as she walked, but she had a proud stride. She'd said she was recovering from a little injury. He wondered what happened. It sure didn't seem to slow her down much.

He was glad she'd stopped by. He'd enjoyed her company. Enjoyed it a lot. Not to mention the cinnamon rolls had been a nice bonus.

He turned and looked at the house. He'd told her he'd have it finished by the wedding, but that would take a lot of work. He'd have to put in long hours. Not that he minded long hours. He'd dropped into bed exhausted last night after finishing the plumbing.

Too tired to worry. Too tired to dream. Which suited him just fine.

After he set this last support post, he was going to head back inside and make a master list of everything that needed to be done and sort it out by day so he'd keep on schedule. He didn't want to disappoint Lillian. He was tired of disappointing people...

His phone rang, and he grabbed it from his pocket. "Mel, what did you find out? Anything? Did you find him?"

He listened to the private investigator's answer and wasn't pleased.

"I don't care what it costs. I want you to find him. I want to see him face-to-face."

Mel assured him that everything possible was being done, then they hung up.

He walked out on the beach to the water's edge, staring out into the vast sea, out across the endless water.

Where had Brian gone?

All he knew was he would make it his life's mission to find him.

CHAPTER 12

"Ruby, I hope you don't mind. I brought Charlotte and Robin with me." Sara stood on the front porch of Ruby's house with her friends.

Ruby swung open her door. "I don't mind at all. Come in. All of you."

"We wanted to see the plans for the dress." Charlotte hugged Ruby.

"How's that son of mine? I haven't seen him in days," Ruby asked Charlotte as she led them inside.

"He's been busy at the marina. We're having dinner tonight, though," Charlotte said.

"I'm glad he's making more time for you now. He's a stubborn one, my Ben. But the marina—any job—isn't more important than people you care about." Ruby turned and motioned to a large table. "I cleaned the table off. Why don't you lay it out there?"

Sara carefully placed the dress on the table and spread it out.

"It's really pretty," Charlotte said, running her hand over the lace. "I love the detail in the lace."

Ruby picked up a large sketch pad. "Here are some designs I sketched. We can change anything, but these were some ideas I had."

They all leafed through the sketches, one by one.

"Sara? Which do you like?" Robin asked.

"This one." Sara pointed to a sleeveless design with a simple, scooped neckline.

Charlotte grinned. "Good, because that's my favorite and you'll look fabulous in it."

Sara was pleased. She'd always admired Charlotte's sense of style. From easy bohemian to pulling together a simple, elegant style. If Charlotte thought this would suit her for the wedding, she was sure it would.

"I'll be able to leave the back of the dress with all the lace-covered buttons." Ruby fingered a delicate button on the dress. "I could take in a bit of the fullness in the skirt portion. I think that might look nice."

"I like that idea." Sara nodded and looked at Charlotte who also nodded her agreement.

"And you like the knee-length instead of full-length?"

"I do. Especially since we're having the ceremony out on the beach."

"Perfect. Let's get some measurements." Ruby grabbed her tape measure and took measurements while Robin wrote them all down for her.

When Ruby finished, Sara hugged her. "Ruby, I can't thank you enough."

"Oh, I'm happy to do it. I'll call you as soon as I'm ready for your first fitting."

"Oh, I want to come to that." Charlotte's eyes lit up.

"Of course." Ruby nodded.

Charlotte dropped Sara and Robin off back at the inn before heading home to work on her newest painting.

"Now I have to meet with Jay about the food. You want to come?"

"Sure." Robin headed to the kitchen and Sara trailed behind her, glancing at her notebook as they walked.

They found Jay and Lillian in the kitchen, sitting at a table in the corner. "Jay was just making some suggestions on what we could serve." Lillian looked up, pen in hand, with a pad of paper sitting in front of her.

Sara and Robin joined them at the table. "Noah said for me to decide on food, but he is going with me to Julie's tomorrow to test some cakes. He'd never pass up a chance to sample Julie's baking." Sara grinned, then looked at Jay. "So, give me your ideas for a menu."

They sat for an hour, discussing pros and cons of different items until they came up with a menu that everyone was happy with.

"You'll need to give me an idea of how many people are coming." Jay set his pen down. "So I'll know how much to order."

"I'll get the invitations out in the next few days. Charlotte and I ordered them today and put in for rush shipping. But I don't know for sure how many will even be on the list. Noah is working on his part. It's getting a bit… bigger… than I planned. I'm not sure how soon we'll know who is actually coming." She bit her lip at the uncertainty of so many details about the wedding.

"Give me the final number you invite. We'll

be able to fudge things a bit since it'll be a buffet. I'll order in extra supplies. We can always use them for the dining room at the inn."

"You're the best, Jay." Sara sighed a long breath of relief. Another thing checked off the mile-long to-do list.

"So they say." Jay grinned.

"Don't encourage him." Robin shook her head, but a smile tilted the corners of her mouth.

Sara wanted to roll her eyes at both Jay and Robin. Someday they would do something about how they felt about each other. Maybe. If either one of them would ever admit it. To themselves or to each other.

Jay watched Lillian and Sara leave, still talking about wedding details. Who knew so much was involved in planning weddings? Robin still sat at the table with him, sipping a glass of iced tea.

"You're really good at pulling together menus with great food pairings," Robin said.

"It's nothing." He brushed the compliment aside, but it pleased him that Robin thought that.

"No, you really are. From planning a menu for weddings to varying the menu for the dining room."

He shifted uncomfortably in his seat.

"But you're lousy at taking compliments." She grinned.

"Am not."

"Are so."

He stared at the smile that spread across Robin's face. She had a faint smattering of freckles and her hair was pulled back, though he admitted to himself he preferred it when she wore it down, brushing her shoulders. Not that it mattered to him how she wore her hair, of course.

"Now that we have your lack of grace at accepting compliments confirmed, my work is done." She stood. "I should go. I have *actual* work to do regarding the inn, even though it seems like planning this wedding is taking up the majority of my time."

"And yet, you don't mind," he said softly.

"No, I don't mind a bit. I love seeing Sara this happy." Robin gave him another small smile and left the kitchen.

He got up and stretched. The emptiness of the space surrounded him even though being alone in the kitchen was pretty much his happy place. Robin always seemed to leave a void when she left, though.

That was just a silly, crazy thought though, wasn't it? He shook his head and walked over to the fridge, pulling out items he needed to get started on the dinner prep. Enough of these absurd thoughts. Back to work.

GARY TURNED from where he was adjusting a cabinet door that didn't close correctly to see Lillian standing at the screen door, a bag in her hand. "Lillian." He closed the cabinet door, pleased to see it finally closed correctly.

"I know you didn't come get dinner because I worked the dining room tonight. So... I brought it to you." She paused. "Unless you already had dinner somewhere?"

He walked over and swung open the screen door. "You didn't need to do that, and I haven't eaten."

"Well, you have to eat."

"I guess I got busy and lost track of time."

"If you don't mind... I brought my dinner, too. I thought we could go over what still needs to be finished here at Magnolia House while we eat."

"That sounds like a plan." He cleared away the papers on the table. How had he made such a mess in such a short time?

He got out some plates and silverware and set the table.

Lil unpacked the bag, grinning when she pulled out a bottle of wine. "You a wine drinker?"

"I am." He turned to rummage through the cabinets and pulled out two mismatched wine glasses.

"George and Ida left some of their dinnerware and glassware. They moved into a much smaller retirement place. I bought some of their extra furnishings. I still need to inventory the kitchen and see what else we'll need to rent the place."

"I'm not sure what all you need, or I'd do it for you," he offered.

"I'll come over one day soon and do it."

That suited him just fine. He liked it when she came to visit. And today had been his lucky day. Twice in one day. They sat down at the table and he poured them both a glass of the red wine.

"Jay made his famous pot roast, so that's what I brought. Hope it's okay."

He took a bite. "It's delicious."

"*Everything* Jay makes is delicious. He's working with a fairly new hire to help him and teaching the new cook how to make the recipes. I'm not sure how well that's working out, because Jay doesn't really like other people working in his kitchen." She smiled.

A smile that lit her eyes and made him feel welcome. Made him feel like he was her friend. Made him feel…

He should quit over analyzing things.

They ate their meal, and he switched his thoughts to the rehab project and told her what his plans were for finishing the house.

"Sounds like you have it all organized." Lillian finally pushed back from the table.

"I hope so." And he hoped he could get it all finished in time. He *would* get it finished in time. Lillian was depending on him.

He turned to a sound at the screen door. "There you are again, pup." He got up to fix the dog his meal. He slowly opened the screen door, and this time the dog only stepped back a pace or two. Placing the bowls down on the stoop, he stood there a moment. "You should try this. It's really good. I bet you'll like it." He murmured words to the dog.

The dog looked at him and slowly crept up to the bowl and ate all the food. After lapping the water, the dog returned to the far edge of the stoop, eyeing him.

Lillian came to the doorway. "Looks like he's getting more used to you," she said softly.

"Hope so."

The pup gave him one more look, one look at Lillian, and then trotted off into the night.

He watched the dog disappear, then turned and came back inside.

"Let me help with the dishes," Lillian offered.

"No, you brought the meal, the least I can do is clean up. But… if you have time…" He didn't know why he was so nervous. That was silly. "We could sit out here and finish our wine?"

"I'd like that."

He grabbed their wine glasses, and they went out on the large stoop by the side door. A lone glider was their only seating choice. They sat next to each other, and he handed Lillian her glass.

He slowly pushed the glider in a soothing,

gentle movement. "The nights here sure are nice. Warm. So many stars." He looked up at the endless array of stars stretched above them.

"They are. In the summer, nights can be hopelessly muggy unless we get a good breeze off the sea. But this time of year, the nights are usually perfect."

He couldn't imagine a night nicer than this. Nice dinner. Good company. Perfect weather.

A sudden surge of guilt overwhelmed him. Why did he deserve a perfect evening like this?

He didn't. It was that simple.

He considered downing his wine in a few big gulps and calling it a night. And yet—it was so nice sitting here with Lillian.

"I don't know what I would have done if you hadn't shown up and offered to finish this job." Lillian looked at him, her eyes warm, and her face held an honest look of appreciation. "It's been such a help. I mean, I would have found someone, eventually. I guess. But now it will all be finished before Sara's wedding, and the work you're doing is very…" She laughed. "It appears you're about as picky about details as I am. I noticed the cabinet doors in the kitchen all hang straight now."

He smiled at her. "I did a few adjustments, yes." He was pleased she'd noticed the cabinets.

They sat and stared at the stars, enjoying their wine, slowly gliding back and forth. She had no idea how much this job meant to him. How much he appreciated the full days of work. The chance to work with his hands. The chance to make sure things were done correctly. He should be thanking her, not her thanking him.

They glided back and forth a few more times while he took a deep breath, gathering his courage. "So I was thinking. Do you think I could take you out to dinner? Tomorrow or sometime when it's convenient for you? I mean, you keep bringing me meals. I'd like to repay the kindness."

"Oh, meals are part of the bargain I made with you."

"I'd still like to repay you." Actually, he'd *like* to take her out. Like on a date. But he didn't put it that way.

She looked at him for a few moments. "Well, okay. If it would make you feel better. And I haven't gone anywhere besides the dining room at the inn in ages."

"Perfect. Does tomorrow night work out for you?"

"It does." She nodded.

"Where would you like to go? You know the places here."

"I always love going to Magic Cafe."

"Then that's where we'll go. I'll come to the lobby of the inn about six?"

"That's perfect. We can walk there if you like. It's not far." She laughed. "Nothing is very far away on the island."

"That's sounds great. It's a date."

Lillian's eyes widened the slightest bit when he made that remark. He should have used a different phrase…

CHAPTER 13

Noah and Jay sat at The Lucky Duck, sipping on beer. "Ben said he'd join us after his dinner with Charlotte. Oh, and there's Del." Jay waved to Delbert Hamilton just entering the tavern.

Noah wasn't sure how Del had slipped into their boys' night out routine. He came from money and ran the Hamilton Hotel chain. But Del and Jay had become friends and soon he'd joined them when Noah, Jay, and Ben got together.

Del slipped onto a stool beside them and ordered a beer. "Kind of a slow night here, isn't it?"

"That's the nice thing about off-season. Not as crowded." Noah absently grabbed some nuts from the bowl on the counter. He might as well enjoy this night out with "the boys." As near as he could figure, every moment of the next few weeks was filled with wedding prep.

"Evidently the guests at the inn didn't get the notice about off-season. We're nearly booked solid these days. Which is good for Lillian, I guess. And we got the cottages all rehabbed and updated now, so there are more rooms. And we'll have the Magnolia House when that Gary guy gets it finished."

"How's that going?" Delbert asked.

"Everything I've seen of his work is spot on. Precise. Good craftsmanship." Rare praise from Jay.

"That's good. Lillian doesn't need the kind of work I heard Vince was doing," Noah said. "Though Vince is gossiping about Lillian around town. Bad-mouthing her for firing him. Says he's losing business because of it."

"Anyone who knows Lil won't listen to him, and he's losing business because he's unreliable and does shoddy work. He was a bad hire. But this Gary guy is working out for her."

Ben slid onto a stool next to them. "Here I am. Charlotte was tired tonight and went home early. Too much wedding planning, I think." He let out a long sigh. "Hey, Del. Good to see you. Jay. And Noah, my friend, you really messed things up for me."

Noah looked at him. "Me? What did I do?"

"Well… you see…" Ben dug into his pocket and took out a box. "I'd gotten this ring for Charlotte." He popped open the box. "Was going to ask her to marry me this weekend when we'd planned an outing to Blue Heron Island on Lady Belle." He slid the box back into his pocket. "But… well, now the timing is off. You asked Sara to marry you and you have the wedding in four weeks. I want Charlotte to feel special when I ask her. I mean… I don't know what I mean. I just think she'd feel like her engagement was overshadowed. Or that she'd feel bad taking away some of the spotlight from Sara."

Noah laughed. "The sad thing? I kinda followed your logic there, buddy. Not that I'm apologizing for asking Sara to marry me or having the wedding so soon. Can't wait to marry her."

"No, of course not. I just think… with the girls being so close…" Ben let out a long sigh. "Anyway, I'll just keep the ring until after your wedding and plan something special for when I ask her."

"Wow, the bachelor population around here is going to get sparse." Jay grinned and took a sip of his beer.

"You could always ask Robin out. You know. Go on a date." Ben eyed Jay.

"What? Nah, we're just friends. Nothing like that."

"If you say so," Noah said, only partially under his breath. He flagged Willie. "A beer for my friend here. To cheer him up."

Willie brought Ben a beer and Noah raised his glass. "To engagements and weddings. May we all survive them."

His friends laughed, but Noah knew, deep inside, that he was as excited about his upcoming wedding as Sara was. He couldn't wait until they were husband and wife. Or wife and husband. Or whatever was the proper way to say it these days.

Married. He was finally marrying the woman he'd loved for decades. Even if for part of that time, he'd not really known it, or at least hadn't acknowledged it.

"My drinking buddies are sure going to be cut back soon." Jay scowled.

"I'll still meet up with you in my semi-bachelor state." Delbert raised his glass.

"Not sure you're really a bachelor after years of dating Camille." Jay shook his head.

"No ring though. I think he qualifies as a bachelor," Noah disagreed.

"I'm pretty sure we'll still be able to make time for you, buddy." Ben raised his glass and clinked Jay's.

"You mean you'll make time besides coming to the kitchen at the inn and swiping cookies?"

"I still plan on doing that." Ben's face twitched in a smile, then he frowned. "But I haven't even asked Charlotte yet, and we don't even know what her answer will be. I think things are going great between us, but we did have a rocky time there for a bit." He looked at Jay and Noah.

Noah held his hands up. "Don't look at me. Sara hasn't said a word either way about you two."

"Robin hasn't either," Jay added.

Del grinned. "I'm pretty sure I'm not up on the inside scoop on you and Charlotte."

"Then, that's probably good news? Like maybe I've fixed my screwups?" Ben shook his head. "This dating thing is complicated."

Noah clapped him on the back. "Wait until you see how complicated getting married is, my friend."

~

LILLIAN CRAWLED IN BED, tired from the long day. She reached for the leather journal sitting on the night table. "What can you tell me? Who wrote all about their life in here?"

Here she was, talking to a journal like an old crazy lady.

She smiled as she adjusted the pillows again and leaned back. But before she could open the journal, her thoughts hopscotched over to Gary. He was taking her to dinner. And he'd said "it's a date." But that was just an expression. Right? He said it was just to repay her for bringing meals over to him. Repay her kindness.

But... had it just been kindness? Hadn't she really wanted to join him in the meals? But only so they could discuss work. Right?

But even if it wasn't a date-date, how long had it been since she'd gone to dinner with a man? She couldn't even remember the last time. She had always been so busy with first raising Sara and running the inn. Then after Sara left and moved to Boston, there was still the inn and it had gotten busier and busier. And the random dates she had were... less than stellar. Who had time for dating, anyway? Besides, she was set in her ways now. Used to being single.

But she *was* looking forward to going to dinner with Gary... Which was kind of foolish, wasn't it?

She shook her head and ran her fingers over the smooth, worn leather of the journal, wondering who the young woman might have been who poured her heart into the words. She opened the journal to where she'd left off. No skipping ahead this time. She might miss something.

She read a handful of entries. It was clear the father of the girl writing the journal did not like this Johnny fellow, and it was just as clear that the girl did. She'd snuck off to meet him at the lighthouse one evening but had gotten caught coming back in and told her father she'd been out with Jane.

She closed the journal, determined to make time to go to the historical society and try to figure out who the author was. Placing the journal back on the night table, she reached to switch off the light.

Events of the day cluttered her mind, and she tried to push them away. An hour later she was still wide awake. She debated getting up and making some chamomile tea or sitting up for a while and knitting. But she couldn't quite get the energy to do either of those.

Her last thoughts before she finally drifted to sleep were of Gary and their upcoming date.

CHAPTER 14

Lillian went over to Ruby's late the next morning after helping out in the dining room. She wanted to see the progress on Sara's dress. Or at least that's the excuse she gave herself. But she knew why she really was going. She wanted to talk to her friend about her date with Gary. She was nervous as a schoolgirl about it and that was ridiculous.

She knocked on the screen door to Ruby's house.

Ruby came to open the door. "Come in."

"I wanted to see how things are going with the dress."

"Come into the dining room. I've taken it over with the dressmaking project."

She followed Ruby to the dining room. The dress was taken apart at the waist and the skirt portion was separate now.

"I'm taking in the skirt a bit. Making it not so full. Sara and her mother were about the same size at the waist, so there won't be much alteration there."

"How did you ever learn how to do all this?" Lillian looked at the project in admiration and then at her talented friend.

"I taught myself. I just really enjoy the process." Ruby shrugged. "Now, how about we have a cup of tea?"

"I'd love that."

Ruby put on the teakettle and they sat at the kitchen table, waiting for the water to boil.

"How's Magnolia House coming along?" Ruby asked.

"Funny you should ask that. It's coming along great. Gary says he'll have it finished before the wedding so we can use it for guests."

"That's nice."

"And…" She fidgeted with the bracelet on her wrist. "And Gary asked if he could take me to dinner. He said it was because I've been bringing him meals and he wants to repay me."

"That's nice of him."

"You don't think it's really... well... it's not really a date, is it?"

"I don't know. He asked you to dinner. That sounds pretty much like a date to me."

"Maybe..." She frowned. "No, I think it's strictly because, as he said, he wants to repay my kindness."

"How about you don't worry about what to call it and just go and enjoy yourself?"

Lillian laughed. "That's the most sensible suggestion I've heard. Where were you when I couldn't sleep last night trying to decide what this thing tonight was called?"

"Ah, one of those nights? I have them often. The ones where I can't turn my mind off."

"Yes, it was one of those nights. I was reading the journal and got tired. But as soon as I switched off the light, my mind started racing with wedding plans and thoughts about Gary."

"Did you find out anything else about who wrote the journal?"

"No other clues, but I'm forcing myself to read it sequentially. We'll see if anything else shows up. Whoever wrote it does have a thing for this Johnny person. And her father doesn't like him. But I still need to get to the historical society and do some research."

"How about we go after our tea? Do you have time? I'd love to help."

She looked at her watch. "I do. And I have to admit my curiosity is getting the best of me. Maybe we can solve the mystery."

Ruby and Lillian walked into the historical society and Etta Swenson greeted them. "Ruby, Lil, haven't seen you two in a while."

"Hi, Etta. We're here to do some research. I found—well, it wasn't actually me who found it —anyway, there's this journal. It was found in the Magnolia House. You know the one, beside the inn?"

"I heard you bought it for a guest house." Etta nodded.

"The journal is from 1898 and forward. I'm trying to find out who wrote it. Maybe give it back to her family if I can find them."

"How can I help?"

"Do you have newspapers dating back that far? To 1898?"

"Just a few. Most got damaged in a couple of hurricanes that hit the area."

"This would have been June of 1898. There was a Sandcastle Festival and this girl and her two friends won it. Noah said that sometimes in the old papers, there were write-ups of things like the festival. I'm hoping it might have full names of the winners."

"Let me go check and see if we have anything. Some things were transcribed or we have scans or copies of them." Etta turned to head to a back room.

"I hope she can find something," Lillian said. "I admit I'm getting more determined to find out who wrote this. I even want to find out if she ended up with this Johnny character."

About five minutes later, Etta came out of the backroom. "I'm sorry. It doesn't look like we have anything from that time."

"Well, it was a long shot. I was just hoping for a clue. Maybe I'll find out something else as I'm reading the journal."

"If you do, and I can help you, just let me know." Etta smiled at them. "I'd love to help you solve the mystery."

"Me too. I find the whole mystery so intriguing," Ruby added.

"Thanks. I'll come by if I find anything else that might help."

"I'm sorry you couldn't find anything," Ruby said as they left.

"I am, too." Disappointment swept through Lillian, unsure if she would ever figure out who wrote the journal.

"Maybe you'll get some more clues as you read along."

"I hope so." Lillian sighed and then scowled to see the woman approaching them.

"Hello, Lillian, Ruby." Camille Montgomery's face held a fake smile.

Lillian just barely kept herself from groaning, not a very charitable reaction to seeing the woman. "Camille, so lovely to see you." *Did that sound sincere?*

"I heard the news that Sara is getting married in just four weeks. Did she have to get married? You know, because... well, is there a baby on the way?" Camille lowered her voice to a conspiratorial whisper.

"Camille, really?" Ruby's voice held an accusing tone.

"What? *No.* They just didn't want to wait long for the wedding." Not that it was any of Camille's business, but the last thing they needed was for her to go around town spreading gossip.

"I guess we'll all find out soon enough, won't we?"

"Camille, don't you go spreading rumors," Ruby threatened, protective of Sara's reputation.

"Oh, no. *Of course* not." Camille's smile said otherwise. "I guess I'll see you at the wedding." She turned and walked away.

Lillian was fairly confident that Camille was *not* on the wedding guest list…

Ruby turned to her. "That woman…"

"I know. I try to be kind to her, but she is just so…"

"So impossible. She better not go spreading rumors about Sara or she can answer to me."

"And me." Lillian nodded, staring off in the direction Camille headed, watching her walk away in her dress that had not one wrinkle and heels. *Heels. Impossibly high heels.* She looked down at her own sensible, sturdy sandals.

"She does like to meddle and spread rumors." Ruby sighed. "I'm going to run to the market and get something for dinner. I hope you have a good time with Gary tonight."

"Thanks. I do, too. If I don't freak myself out overthinking the whole thing."

Ruby laughed. "Stop it."

Lillian smiled. "A wise friend told me to just go and enjoy myself."

"Your friend is very wise, indeed." Ruby grinned and headed down the sidewalk.

Lillian stood there for a moment, lost in thought. She pulled herself out of it and hurried off toward the inn. She still had a lot to do before her dinner with Gary tonight.

LILLIAN WALKED into the kitchen at The Nest after getting ready for dinner with Gary. Sara sat at the table, working on her laptop, and looked up when she came into the room.

"You look nice," Sara said. "What's the occasion? Going out with some of The Yarn Society ladies?"

And that was a problem, too, wasn't it? Sara wouldn't ever even think that she was going out on a date. "I'm..." She shrugged. "I'm going to Magic Cafe with Gary."

Sara's eyes widened. "You're going on a date?"

"Kinda?"

"That's wonderful."

"It's not that big of a deal."

"I think it is. I can't remember the last time I've seen you go on a date." Sara frowned. "Have I ever?"

"I'm sure you have." Maybe? Men had asked her out. It wasn't that. It was just she automatically turned them down. Almost always. She was too busy. Or not interested.

Or... scared of change?

So why had she said yes to Gary when she was actually busier than usual and to be honest, it did scare her a little?

Sara got up and hugged her. "I hope you have a great time."

"I'm sure it will mostly be just talking business. Discussing his work on Magnolia House."

"Maybe you should make it less business and just enjoy yourself."

"That's what Ruby said. Anyway, I should go." She reached for her cell phone and slipped it in her pocket. "I said I'd meet him in the lobby."

Sara grinned. "I feel like I should stalk behind you and watch from the shadows, like a mother watching her kid catch the school bus for the first time."

She laughed. "You just stay here and work. I'll be fine." If she could just get over being so nervous. Taking a deep breath, she set her shoulders, left The Nest, and headed to the lobby.

CHAPTER 15

Gary stood in the lobby of Charming Inn. Well, he wasn't exactly standing. He paced back and forth, waiting for Lillian, glancing at his watch. Though he'd gotten here early. She wasn't late.

He turned from his pace-track and saw her standing there. She looked... beautiful. She had on a simple, casual red dress that looked stunning on her. She'd clipped her hair back on one side with a silver hair-thingy.

Crossing the room, he paused in front of her, gathering his thoughts and hoping he didn't look like a fool. "You look lovely."

She blushed at the compliment. "Thank you."

They stood there awkwardly for a moment

before he finally found words. "I… uh… should I drive us over?"

"It's not far. Would you like to walk?"

"Yes, that sounds perfect if it's okay with you." Maybe walking would give him time for some of his nervous energy to fade away. Maybe. Hopefully.

As they left, he noticed Lillian's niece standing near a far entranceway talking to another young woman standing there. She was glancing their direction but trying to act like she wasn't. He smiled at her and gave a little wave. Lillian seemed totally unaware her niece was watching her leave.

"She's on a date?" Robin's eyes widened.

"Sh. Stand still. Don't look. I don't want her to see me watching her." Sara grabbed her friend's hand and turned her away from the departing couple. "But I had to come see this. Aunt Lil getting picked up for a date."

"Jay says that Gary fellow is a nice enough guy. Doing good work on Magnolia House."

"I hope he is. But really, can you remember Aunt Lil going out on a date?"

Robin's forehead creased. "I... well, now that you ask, I can't remember her dating someone. She's just always been so independent."

"And alone." Sara frowned. "She gave up so much to raise me."

"And I'm sure she loved every minute of it. You're her world, you know."

"I just want her to be happy." Sara stared off to where Aunt Lillian and Gary had been standing.

"I'm pretty sure Lillian is one of the happiest, most content woman I've ever known."

"But I'll be moving out to live with Noah after we're married. I don't want her to be lonely."

"She lived alone when you went to college and while you were in Boston. That's a lot of years."

"And I always worried about her being alone."

"Lillian is rarely alone. She has her friends. She has the inn."

Sara sighed. "I just think it would be so fabulous if she'd fall in love."

"Whoa, girlfriend. She's just going out to dinner."

"I know. But maybe this will be the first of her dating people. Breaking the ice, so to speak."

"Maybe. I just hope she has a good time. She deserves a night out."

"That she does. Between running the inn and working on wedding stuff, she's been super busy."

"Busy is exactly how Lillian likes to be." Robin grabbed her hand. "Come on, let's go get a glass of wine and sit on the deck. We can work on the wedding planning."

Sara gave one last glance at the door where Aunt Lillian had been and turned to follow her friend.

TALLY GREETED Lillian and Gary at Magic Cafe and sat them at a table near the beach. "The grouper is on special tonight." She handed them menus. "I'll send Tereza over to get your orders."

"Thanks, Tally."

Gary leaned close across the table. "Everyone in town knows you, don't they?"

She laughed. "Pretty much."

Gary leaned back and looked around the restaurant. "This is nice. I love how there's seating right out here at the edge of the beach."

"It is nice. The food is wonderful, too."

"And look at the view we have. The gulf is just right there." Gary swung a hand toward the water. "This is just perfect."

It was a perfect setting and Tally always made her feel so welcome. If she could just get over feeling so... nervous. Lost. Clueless.

How *did* one act on a date?

Lillian opened her menu, though she was fairly certain she'd have the grouper special. And hushpuppies. Magic Cafe had great hushpuppies. If she concentrated on reading each item on the menu, though, maybe it would settle her nerves.

Gary set down his menu. "I'm going to try the grouper special."

She looked up from where she'd been pretending to read the menu. "I think I will, too."

Tereza came over. "Hi, Lillian. Haven't seen you in a long time."

Gary grinned and gave her a see-I-told-you-everyone-knows-you look.

"Tereza, this is Gary. He's doing some work on Magnolia House for me."

"Oh, George and Ida's house. I'd heard you bought it." Tereza turned to Gary with her always-welcoming smile. "Nice to meet you."

"Nice to meet you."

"Have you two decided what you'd like to order?"

"We're both going to have your grouper special." Gary eyed her to make sure she was still in agreement. "And how about a bottle of wine?"

"That sounds nice."

"We have a new Italian pinot grigio from the Alto Adige region. It's very good."

"Sounds good to me. Lillian?" Gary tilted his head and looked at her.

"Yes, that sounds lovely."

Tereza left and Lillian no longer had her menu to hide behind so she caught herself fidgeting with the silverware.

Gary let out a long sigh, and she looked at him. His mouth curved into a small smile. "I'm just so darn nervous. Silly, isn't it? Because you've always been easy to talk to, but tonight I can't find my words. But I don't ask women out very often and… well, I'm just yammering now, aren't I?" He laughed.

She let out her own long sigh. "I'm a bit nervous myself. I don't really date often. Like hardly ever." Like she couldn't remember the last time, but she wasn't going to share that exactly.

"Is it wrong that it makes me feel better that you're nervous, too?" He grinned.

She laughed and her nervousness began to fade slowly away like a retreating wave slipping down the beach.

And just like that, the mood changed, and they had a nice dinner, chatting about this and that. They sat at the end of the meal, finishing their wine.

"That was seriously a fabulous meal." Gary leaned back in his chair, holding his wineglass.

"It was. It's always a good meal here." She looked out toward the beach. "Do you think you'd like to walk back the beach way Charming Inn? I think we could catch the sunset if we did that."

"I think that's a wonderful idea. I can't get enough of your sunsets here on the island. They are spectacular."

They finished their drinks, said goodbye to Tereza and Tally. Tally hugged her. "Don't be a stranger."

As they were leaving, she spied Camille and her boyfriend, Delbert Hamilton, coming into the restaurant. She tugged on Gary's arm, hoping to hurry out and avoid them.

No such luck. Camille waltzed up to them. "Well, well, Lillian. Twice in one day. Are you already *finished* with dinner? How early did you eat?" Camille shook her head in a clearly disapproving manner. "I swear, people down here on Belle Island are just so… *provincial*."

"Yes, we were just leaving." She grabbed Gary's arm to turn him toward the steps to the beach.

"Who is this?" Camille looked at Gary and gave him a wide, charming smile. "I'm Camille Montgomery, and this is Delbert Hamilton, of Hamilton Hotels."

Delbert held out a hand to Gary.

"Um, this is Gary Jones." Lillian introduced Gary.

The men shook hands and Delbert looked at Gary closely as if searching his face for some kind of recognition.

"Gary is working on rehabbing the house I bought next to the inn."

That seemed to satisfy Delbert's curious look, and he smiled.

"Delbert, I think I told you that Lillian's niece is getting married in just four weeks. You know, kind of in a *hurry*." Camille had a perfectly innocent look on her face, but Lillian didn't miss what she implied.

"Congrats to the couple," Delbert said.

"Delbert talked me into coming here for dinner. I keep telling him he should open a hotel here on the island and put in a great dining room there so there would be a nice place to eat on the island."

"Camille, there are great places to eat here. Like at Charming Inn. Can't ask for a better chef than Jay."

"But the place lacks… atmosphere." Camille shrugged.

"We should go." Lillian didn't even try to act cordial anymore.

"I love the dining room at Charming Inn. Competes with some of the finest meals I've had in Seattle, and we have some great restaurants there," Gary defended her. Or her inn. Or maybe Jay.

A strange look flitted across Gary's face and Delbert looked at him closely again, then said, "I'd agree with that. Great food."

"We'll let you get to your dinner." This time she took hold of Gary's arm and firmly led him away toward the beach. Before she said something rude to Camille. Not that anything she could say could compete with Camille's rude remarks.

CHAPTER 16

Gary chastised himself every step down the stairs and out onto the sand. He wasn't sure if that Delbert guy had recognized him, though he hadn't said anything. And why in the world had he mentioned Seattle? He'd so far managed to just vaguely remark about the west coast. Now he'd gone and blurted out the city where he lived. Sooner or later, the truth was going to come out.

"That Camille. I don't really take to her much." Lillian's words interrupted his thoughts.

"She's rather—I don't know the word for her."

"Rude?"

"I wasn't going to say that." He laughed. "Okay, maybe I was."

"That's what she is. Always so full of herself. Putting on airs. And I swear, if she goes around spreading rumors about Sara *having* to get married, she'll to have to deal with me."

"Having to get married?"

Lillian sighed. "You know, like if Sara was pregnant, and they were rushing to get married before the baby. Or before she looked pregnant or whatever. Which isn't the case, but Camille loves to spread gossip, true or false."

"I'm sorry."

"Maybe Camille will head back home before she does much damage. She's from Comfort Crossing, Mississippi, but I believe she moved to Mobile now. Anyway, if she'd decide it was time to head North, you'd get no complaints from me."

"And that Delbert runs Hamilton Hotels?"

"He does. Took over most of it from his father, I believe. But his father is still involved in the business."

So how would Delbert have recognized him? Because he was fairly certain the man had. Of course, his name and photo had been splashed in the news. Maybe that was it. And Delbert was in the hotel business...

"Anyway,   enough   complaining   about

Camille, let's enjoy our walk." Lillian slipped off her shoes.

He followed her example, pushing worries about Delbert from his mind. For now.

They headed down the beach. The sand had cooled as the sun had faded, and they crossed to the water's edge. The water lapped at their feet and ankles as they walked down the beach.

Gary stopped and reached down to pick up a shell. He turned and smiled at her. "I'm a shell seeker."

"Oh, I'm always picking up a shell or two on my beach walks. Not that I don't have bowls and clear vases of them all over my home. Still always seem to find one I just *need*."

He slipped the shell in his pocket and they continued down the beach. The sky darkened into shades of orange and they slowed their pace. "Do you want to just sit on the beach and watch the sunset?" he asked. "I mean, I know you have on a nice dress and everything."

She laughed. "I don't own an outfit that I wouldn't sit on the beach in." She sank down to the sand, and he sat beside her.

They sat quietly as the sunset unfolded before them. A few couples walked by and they'd nod or say hi to them, but mostly, they just sat in silence. She leaned back, her hands in the sand. Gary leaned back, too, and his hand grazed hers. He looked at her and smiled and left his hand just a fraction of an inch from hers on the sand.

LILLIAN SWORE she could feel the heat from Gary's hand, so close to hers. She swore she could feel an electric force, a magnetic force, pulling their hands closer.

"Well, it's getting dark. I guess we should head back." Gary rose, breaking the connection. He reached out a hand.

She reached up and took his hand as he helped her stand. This time she didn't do one of her ridiculous stumbles getting up. Minor victory in the recovery from her injury awhile back.

They headed back toward the inn, and to her horror, she started to stumble not six steps down the beach. He caught her up against him. "You okay?"

She let out an exasperated sigh. "I am. Just… well, it's a bit dark." Not that the dark had anything to do with it. She just didn't have full strength back yet, no matter how hard she worked at it. She always was a bit unsteady right when she got up, and it annoyed her mightily.

He placed her hand on his arm. "How about you just hold on here while we walk?"

She wouldn't admit she needed his arm— and she *didn't*—but she really kind of liked leaving her hand on his arm, connected to him. He rested his hand over hers as they continued to the inn, slowly ambling along the hard-packed sand portion of the beach.

When they got back to the inn, he walked her to The Nest and paused at the bottom of the stairs to her deck.

"I had a fabulous evening with you. I'm glad you let me take you to Magic Cafe." Gary still held his hand over hers.

"I had a good time, too."

"Do you think—" He paused and shuffled his feet in the sand. "Would you like to go out again?"

"I—" She looked at him, wavering on saying yes or saying no. It seemed silly to date a man who was just here on the island for a short time. And yet... she really would like to go out with him again. "Yes, I would." She answered before she could overthink the whole thing.

"Great. Tomorrow night?" He grinned. "Or is that too soon?"

She really should help out on the dinner rush, but it *was* mid-week. "How about I cook for you?" She did love to cook and rarely took the time to do it.

"I'm not going to turn down a home-cooked meal."

"Okay, how about six-thirty tomorrow? Even though Camille would think that is way too early."

Gary laughed. "The time is great for me. I'll see you then."

She took her hand back—reluctantly—and headed up the stairs. She turned and gave him a wave as she slipped inside.

Sara looked up from where she was reading on the couch. "Good, you're home. Tell me everything."

Lillian crossed over and sat beside her. "I don't know what you want to know. We went to Magic Cafe. Then we sat on the beach and watched the sunset. Then he walked me back here to The Nest."

"Did you have a good time? Were you nervous? Did you just talk business?"

Lillian laughed. "Slow down." She leaned back on the couch. "I did have a good time. We talked some business. And yes, I was nervous at first. But then he said he was nervous and then — Then I wasn't."

Sara nodded. "Good. I'm glad you had a good time. Are you going to see him again? I mean like on a date, not like going over to check on Magnolia House."

"It just so happens that he asked me out again. But I offered to cook for him instead. He's coming over to dinner tomorrow night."

Sara grinned. "This is working out nicely."

"It's not really a big deal. I just enjoy his company."

"Whatever you say."

"Really, we're just… I guess we're friends now. Though, that does seem quick to become friends, doesn't it?"

"Nope. Not if you like him."

"I don't *like* him. I mean I *do* like him… but not like that." She shook her head. "Now I'm confusing myself."

"I'm just glad to see you going out and

enjoying yourself. He looked really handsome tonight."

She narrowed her eyes. "How would you know?"

"Oops. Caught me. I might have snuck over to the inn and watched from the distance with Robin while he picked you up."

She laughed. "I guess I'm not surprised."

She grabbed the teal plaid throw and dropped it over her lap, fingering the fringe, debating on telling Sara about running into Camille.

"What?" Sara asked. "I can tell you're thinking about something."

"I—I ran into Camille today. Twice, actually. She's…" Lillian sighed. "I think she's spreading rumors about you and Noah and your wedding. She's implying you have to get married. You know. Because—"

"She thinks I'm pregnant?" Sara laughed. "Won't she feel foolish in a few months when I'm obviously not with child."

"I just thought you should know in case you start hearing the rumor."

"Not even Camille and her silly gossip can faze me. I'm glad Noah and I decided to get married so soon. Camille can gossip away."

"She said she'd see us at the wedding, and I didn't clue her in that she's not on the list." Lillian shook her head.

"Actually…" Sara shrugged. "Delbert is on Noah's list. He's been meeting up with Noah, Jay, and Ben at The Lucky Duck and they've all become friends. So, I guess he'll be bringing Camille as his date."

"I guess that can't be helped, then. But I don't have to like it. If I'm lucky, maybe I won't have to speak to her at the wedding." Lillian let out a small laugh. "But knowing Camille, she'll make a point to come up to me and say something rude. But we won't let anything she says ruin the day."

"We won't." Sara stood up and grabbed her book. "I'm headed for bed. But I'll have Noah take me out to dinner tomorrow so you can have the place to yourself."

"You don't have to do that. You two could join us."

"Maybe next time. I'll let you have time alone with him and get to know him better." Sara leaned down and kissed her on the forehead. "Night, Aunt Lil. Love you."

"Love you too."

Sara left, and she sat there just staring into

the room. She should knit for a while to settle down. Or, better yet, she could get ready for bed and read some more of the journal. Maybe some new clue would come up.

She got up from the couch and headed for bed.

CHAPTER 17

Gary woke up in a great mood. He made coffee and took a cup outside to watch the sunrise. Well, the reflected sunrise since the house faced the west toward the gulf. But the clouds over the water turned a delicate pink as the sun rose in the east. He turned to go back inside and start to work when he spied the pup hanging out near the doorway.

"Hello there, pup." He slowly walked toward the dog. "I'll get your breakfast."

He went inside and got the food, then set it down just inside the doorway. He propped open the door and stepped back. "Come on in, pup."

The dog walked to the doorway and peeked inside, then slowly took the few steps over to the bowl. He scarfed up his food, then sat down beside the bowl.

"I should really give you a name, you know. I can't just keep calling you pup." He held out his hand and the dog slowly got up and walked over and nosed it. "Good boy." He gently petted the dog. "I think I'll call you Rover. You certainly rove around a lot. What do you think of that name?"

The dog tilted his head.

"No? Too obvious?"

"How about Max? That's a good, solid name."

The pup tilted his head the other direction.

"I give up. What do you want me to call you? Lucky? You're kind of lucky that you came to my house and now you get fed regularly, aren't you?"

The dog wagged his tail.

"Ah, so that's what you want your name to be. Lucky it is." He felt ridiculously happy to have named the pup and a bit foolish for looking to the dog for its opinion.

"I've got to get to work now. You want to hang around? Come on outside. I'm working on the deck." He grabbed his toolbox and headed outside with Lucky trotting beside him.

Lucky sat in the shade, watching him work for hours until he looked up one time and the dog was gone.

Hopefully Lucky would come back for dinner, because, after all, he did have a proper name now.

"HEY, Lillian, there's a call for you." Robin held up the phone at the reception desk.

Lillian hurried over and took the phone. "Hello?"

"Lillian, this is Etta. I know we couldn't find a paper from the time frame you wanted, but I got to thinking. The town paper used to print a Fifty Years Ago and a One Hundred Years Ago section. It's a long shot, but maybe we could find something in one of those columns in a newer paper."

"Oh, that would be wonderful." Lillian glanced at her watch. She had time before lunch to run to the historical society. "I'll be over in a few minutes."

"I'll be here."

"Still looking to find out who wrote the journal?" Robin asked.

"I am. Etta had some more ideas. I'm going to run over there now. I'll be back before the lunch crowd hits."

"Good luck."

She headed to The Nest to grab the journal, then went to the Historical Society. Etta greeted her as she entered. "I hope this works. Maybe we can find some kind of clue."

Lillian wrote down the date of the Sandcastle Festival and they did some quick math to figure out approximately fifty and a hundred years later. Etta looked through some actual paper copies in the back while Lillian looked at digital scans.

Etta came hurrying out of the back storage room. "Look. I found something." She carefully spread the paper out on a large table.

Lillian leaned over the table and looked at the section Etta pointed to. "Fifty years ago. It says that fifty years ago Jane Belle and Clara and Anna Smith won the sandcastle making competition with a sandcastle lighthouse." She turned to Etta. "Look, her friend Jane was a Belle. From the family that founded the island. And do you think Clara and Anna were sisters?"

"Or maybe cousins?" Etta suggested.

"And Smith for a last name. Really? Can't they help me out a little bit more?" Lillian laughed. "But at least I have the writer's name now. Anna Smith." Just knowing the name made her feel better. Anna.

"Do you have any other dates or events we could look into?"

"Not yet, but I'll keep reading and let you know." She glanced at her watch. "But now, I need to leave and get back to work. I really appreciate your help. I'm so glad you thought of these columns."

"Me, too. This is fascinating trying to unravel the mystery." Etta walked her to the door. "Let me know if you find out anything else, and I'll research it for you."

"Thanks, Etta." She slipped outside into the sunshine and hurried back to the inn. After the lunch crowd died down, she needed to get busy making dinner for Gary.

Lunch ran long, with a larger than usual crowd. Then a room on the top floor of the inn got a leak, and she had to clean up the water mess and track down a plumber. Then someone came in to ask about holding an event at the inn and Robin was busy, so Lillian talked with them.

She finally glanced at her watch. She had exactly forty-five minutes to change and make dinner for Gary. That just wasn't going to work.

"What's wrong?" Robin walked up to the reception desk. "I can see from the look on your face that something is."

Lillian set down a stack of papers with a frustrated sigh. "I offered to make dinner for Gary tonight. But then things got crazy here and now I don't have enough time. I guess I'll just call him and cancel. We'll do it another time."

"Sara said you had another date planned with Gary tonight."

"No secrets here." Lillian grinned.

"You could go snag dinner from Jay, throw it in the oven to keep it warm, and enjoy your evening almost as planned," Robin suggested.

She frowned. It wasn't exactly what she'd hoped for. She'd wanted to cook, enjoyed cooking. But there really wasn't time. "That's a good idea. I'll grab something from Jay and still have time to get ready."

A grin spread across Robin's lips. "Good. I don't want to have to explain to Sara how I couldn't keep up with everything happening at the inn today so you could have your date."

Lillian headed to the kitchen to beg dinner from Jay.

CHAPTER 18

G ary got cleaned up and dressed and sat at the table in the kitchen, jotting down notes and waiting for it to be time to walk over to the inn. He didn't want to turn up early and look overly eager, but he sure wasn't going to be late, either.

Scratching at the door caught his attention. Lucky was waiting for him on the stoop. "Come on in. I'll get your dinner before I leave." He opened the door and Lucky trotted in as if it were no big deal. Progress.

He got the dog some food and water. Lucky ate the food, and Gary noticed it wasn't at such a frantic pace as before. More progress.

"Well, pup—I mean *Lucky*. I have a dinner date tonight. I'm headed there now. Sorry I can't sit around and chat with you." He picked up the empty food bowl but put the water bowl on the stoop in case Lucky wandered back by later tonight. He walked out the door and Lucky followed him.

"I have to leave, okay? But you make sure you come back in the morning for breakfast. And if you get thirsty, I'm just going to leave water out for you all the time, okay?"

Lucky wagged his tail. Gary headed down the sidewalk to The Nest. Lucky followed along beside him. "Oh, you want to go on a walk? You're certainly welcome to come along with me."

Gary and Lucky strolled down the sidewalk to the inn and around the side of it to The Nest. Lillian answered his knock.

"I see you brought a friend with you."

Lillian stood in the doorway in a pair of simple black slacks and a teal, collared short-sleeve knit top. She looked lovely. He brought his thoughts from how great Lillian looked—and her warm, welcoming smile—and replied, "Lucky. His name is Lucky. We just decided that today, didn't we, pup?" The dog wagged his tail in reply.

"Why don't you two come in?"

"Lucky, you want to come in and join us?"
The dog followed him inside.

"I have a confession to make." Lillian stood in the kitchen with a slightly guilty look on her face. "I know I invited you for a home-cooked meal, but I got tied up with work stuff at the inn. So... I grabbed some dinner from Jay. I hope that's okay. I have it warming in the oven. I'm sorry, the day just kind of got away from me. I promise I'll make good on my offer for a home-cooked meal."

"That's fine," he assured her. He didn't care who cooked the meal, he just wanted to spend time with her. And that surprised him because it had been a very long time since he'd wanted to spend time with a woman. He was always too busy or too stressed or just not really interested in the women he dated off and on.

He was interested in Lillian, and it had only been a week or so since he'd first met her.

"I opened a bottle of wine to let it breathe if you'd like that. Or there's beer in the fridge," Lillian offered.

"Wine is fine."

"I'll pour us some and we can go outside and unwind for a bit before we eat."

They went outside and Lucky plopped down

beside him at the foot of his chair. He mindlessly petted the dog's head.

"Oh, feels good to be off my feet." Lillian leaned back in her chair and stretched out her legs, then slipped off her shoes. "Looks like Lucky is getting used to you."

"I think so. The next thing I'd like to do is give him a bath. I just didn't want to rush things."

"That's probably a good idea. Take things slowly."

"He sat outside watching me work for most of the morning. I almost finished the deck today. I think it turned out great and I was able to use most of the older floorboards. They were still in good shape. But there's an all-new support system under the deck."

"Oh, I'll have to come see it tomorrow."

He quickly tried to suppress his automatic dopey grin at knowing he'd be seeing her tomorrow, too.

LILLIAN WAS PLEASED she now had a reason to visit Gary tomorrow. Not that she really needed a reason. It was perfectly normal for her to go check on the progress he was making, right? After all, he was working for her, fixing up Magnolia House.

She took a sip of her wine and sighed. "That's really good. Tally recommended it to me."

"Tally from Magic Cafe?"

"Yes, she really knows her wines and finds some of the best wines at reasonable prices. I try and offer different wines here at the inn than she has at her restaurant. Though, I'll freely admit she probably has a better wine list than we do." Why was she just chattering away like this?

Gary took a sip of the wine. "This is good."

She wondered how long they could chat about wine…

Gary leaned back in his chair, resting one tanned arm on the armrest, balancing his glass of wine. "I admire how efficiently you run the inn. And you keep it in really nice shape."

The heat of a blush flushed her face. "Ah… thank you."

"It's easy to see you love the place and love your job."

"I do. Even when it gets a bit crazy like today. Can't imagine doing anything else." She smiled at him. "And how about you? Are you retired now?"

"Not exactly. Just taking a bit of a leave of absence, I guess you'd call it."

He didn't seem eager to talk about it, so she let it drop. Maybe he'd gotten burned out on his job and needed a break. Or maybe he'd saved up his vacation days. Or maybe it was really none of her business. She rose from her chair. "I'll go get dinner on the table. You sit out here and enjoy yourself."

Gary jumped up. "No, I'll come in and help."

They went inside, dished up the food, and sat at the table. She wished she would have thought to get out the candles. But why? It wasn't like this was some big romantic dinner or anything. But candlelight was always so… welcoming. Okay, and romantic. Which this dinner wasn't, she reminded herself yet again.

After dinner they went outside, and she scattered a few mason jars filled with fairy lights around them. They should provide just enough to see each other while they talked since the moon was barely a crescent of light tonight.

"Those are nice." He nodded at the lights.

"I think they're so pretty. I have these, and

some that are in wine bottles. Oh, and one that is in a clear vase I found at a thrift shop. I've really gotten into fairy lights. They put out such a delicate, pretty light." There she was, yammering again. She was sure he wasn't interested in her lighting collection.

The night had cooled a bit, and she shivered.

"Are you cold?"

"A bit. I'll just pop in and get a throw to wrap up in." She grabbed her favorite teal throw, and when she returned, he had settled in the loveseat at the end of the deck. She looked at the space on the loveseat beside him or the chair across from him.

"Come, join me." He patted the spot beside him.

She joined him on the loveseat, acutely aware of how close they were. She settled the throw over their laps and his leg brushed hers. The cozy light from the mason jars and the sparkling stars above made the deck a magical place.

He turned and looked at her for a moment, then took her hand in his and smiled. They sat in silence for a while, looking out over the sea. Even though it wasn't light enough to make out each wave, they could see the white of the waves as they broke near the shore.

"This is nice," he finally said and squeezed her hand.

She liked the feeling of her hand in his. The warmth. The comfortable feeling of just sitting next to him.

He looked at her closely and she saw— something—in his eyes. He leaned a fraction of an inch closer and she held her breath. Was he going to kiss her? Did she want him to? Her heart crashed in her chest just like the waves they'd been watching. His eyes locked with hers.

Then he looked away abruptly at the sound of a door opening.

"Hi Gary, Aunt Lil, hope I'm not interrupting. Just got home and saw the fairy lights out here. Wanted to let you know I'm here." Sara stood by the doorway to the deck.

"Do you want to join us?" Lillian asked, a bit disoriented from jumping from is-he-going-to-kiss-me to greeting her niece.

"No, I'm tired. I'm just going to head to bed."

"Okay, good night. Love you."

"Love you, too. Good night, Gary."

"Night, Sara." Gary's deep voice wrapped

around them as Sara walked back inside.

Lillian sat there wondering if he was going to look at her again with that gaze of anticipation.

"She's right. It's getting late. I should let you get inside." Gary let go of her hand and stood.

She wanted to grab his hand again. Wanted to sit with him. Wanted him… to kiss her. But the moment was gone. She stood and gathered the throw, holding it tightly against her. "You're right. It is getting late." She held back the words she wanted to say. *Stay for a while. Look at me like that again. Kiss me…*

"I'm going to walk back the beach way. I'll see you tomorrow when you come catch up on the progress."

"Okay, see you tomorrow." She watched him walk down the beach with Lucky at his side until the darkness swallowed them up.

Had he been getting ready to kiss her? Had she just imagined the whole thing? She guessed she'd never know. But… she had wanted him too. Which was silly because she'd only known him what? A week? And maybe she'd misread the situation, anyway.

She sighed and headed inside with her confused thoughts taunting her.

CHAPTER 19

Lillian headed over to Magnolia House after helping with the breakfast crowd and working the front desk for a bit. She walked the beach way, and the sand was warm beneath her bare feet. Brilliant blue sky stretched above her, the exact shade that had inspired the sky blue color of a crayon, she was sure. A heavy breeze blew in off the water and tossed her hair around her shoulders as she walked.

Gary was standing on the deck and waved to her as she approached. She was surprised to see he'd finished the deck except for part of the railing. He'd finished the steps leading up to it, too. This would have taken Vince weeks and weeks to do. If he'd even shown up to do it.

She climbed the stairs and Gary put down

the hammer he was using. A wide grin spread across his face and she felt her face break into an answering smile. The sun highlighted the few gray hairs on his head and spread warm light across his chiseled jawline. A navy t-shirt stretched across his broad chest.

"Morning, Lil. Glad you could make it over to see the progress."

Yes, she should ask him to show her everything. She should. She hadn't just come over here so she could see him… stare at him…

He'd tanned up quite a bit since he'd gotten to the island. His skin was no longer that pale shade of Northern as she thought of it. His cheeks were kissed with a light redness from the sunshine.

He looked… good. Very good. Handsome and healthy and— *Oh, for goodness' sake, quit staring at him.*

She broke her glance away and looked over at Lucky, stretched out in the sunshine. The dog wagged his tail once when he saw her looking at him. "You gave him a bath."

Gary grinned. "I did. It was kind of an ordeal, but we got through it. I was afraid he might bolt out of here after the bath, but he came outside to bask in the sun to dry."

She walked over to the dog and knelt down to pet him. "You look very handsome all cleaned up, Lucky."

The dog looked at her with a look she'd swear said 'I know.' She stood back up, holding the railing to make sure she didn't lose her balance.

They both turned at the sound of someone coming up the deck stairs. "George, Ida, how great to see you." She hurried over to greet the couple.

"Gary, this is George and Ida. They owned the house before I bought it."

Gary nodded at them.

"We stopped by the inn to see you and they said you were over here. We got your message. Sorry, we were away on a trip so it took us a bit to get back to you," George said as he walked across the deck, looking at it. "This looks nice. The deck needed new supports. I always meant to get to it the last few years we were here, but just never got around to it." He looked at Gary. "Did you do this?"

"I did."

"You do really nice work."

Lillian was strangely pleased that George approved of Gary's work. That was silly, wasn't it? But she was happy that so many people thought his work was good since she'd just trusted her instincts and hired him on the spot.

Ida turned to Lillian. "So, you found a journal here? Hidden in the wall?"

"Gary did. Want to see where it was hidden?"

Ida nodded. Gary led them all inside and showed them the hidden compartment in the wall.

"Well, I'll be. I've never had any idea that was there." George walked over and peered inside it.

"We have no idea whose journal it could be," Ida said. "Have you figured it out?"

"I have a name. Anna Smith." Lillian nodded. "And she started the journal in 1898. But that's all I have. Oh, and she has a sister, or maybe a cousin, Clara."

"Have you checked on previous owners of the house?" George turned around, rubbing his chin.

"Most of the records—the actual deeds— from that time period are lost. Big storm destroyed them long ago."

"That's too bad." Ida shook her head. "I used

to do some genealogy research. Maybe you could get some information from the census records of the island at that time. You have the author's name and her last name. And maybe Clara is her sister."

"That's a great idea. Why didn't I think of that?"

"Lots of those records are online," Ida said. "You might be able to track her down that way or get another lead."

"I'd really like to find her ancestors and give them this journal. It's such a wonderful piece of history. Seems a shame to let it sit and not find its rightful family." Lillian sighed. "I'll have to keep looking. I appreciate the suggestion to try the census records."

George and Ida walked back through the house, and George admired Gary's handiwork. He pointed to the kitchen cabinets. "Those cabinets were the bane of my existence. Could never get the doors to hang properly. Look at them now. All straight."

Ida walked over and clasped Gary's hand. "You kept so much the same. But you've put so much work into it. It's beautiful. The woodwork shines. It reminds me of when we first bought the place. I was afraid you'd rip out the old worn floors and woodwork and modernize it. But the house looks lovely now."

"Honestly, as we got older, it was hard to keep up with everything. Part of the reason we sold it to Lillian and moved to a retirement village on the mainland to be closer to our daughters," George added. "We do miss living on the island, though."

Gary smiled at both of them. "It's a good house. Good structure. I enjoy working on it."

"We should head out." George took Ida's arm and they all headed back outside. He turned to Lillian. "This makes me feel good that you're fixing the place up. Glad we sold it to you. I wish the best for you on using it as a guest house for the inn."

"Thanks, George."

George and Ida headed out to their car. George had Ida's hand in his, then stopped and opened the car door for her. Ida waved as they pulled away.

Lillian turned to Gary. "Nice couple. I do miss having them here as neighbors."

"But at least you got the house to use when they decided to sell."

"And at least I found the perfect person to fix it up for me."

Gary beamed with the compliment. "I'm trying my best to get it all fixed up by the wedding, exactly how you want it."

For the first time, she was almost disappointed the house would be ready by then. Because when the house was finished, what would Gary do? Would he head back home?

CHAPTER 20

The next week flew by in a flurry of wedding planning and Magnolia House rehab. Lillian and Gary got into a routine of having a late dinner every night at the dining room of the inn and going over everything he'd done that day. Charlotte had gone over to the house and picked out paint colors and Gary had ordered the paint they needed.

"That's a lot of work to do all that painting." Lillian said as they sat after dinner one night.

"A lot of hours, yes. And I still need to repair some woodwork and finish up the downstairs bath."

Robin and Sara walked up to the table. "You two still talking about Magnolia House?" Sara asked.

"They're always talking about Magnolia House. Unless we drag her away for wedding planning." Robin laughed.

"Do you need me for something for the planning?" Lillian asked.

"No, just dropping by to say hi. We're headed over to my bungalow to meet Charlotte," Robin assured her. "How's Magnolia House coming along? Haven't been over there in over a week to see it."

"We were discussing painting. Charlotte picked the colors, but it's a lot of work to paint it all."

"How about we have a painting party?" Sara's eyes lit up. "This weekend. I'm sure Noah would help. We'll ask Charlotte—she's the best painter of all of us."

"We'll let Sara roll the middle of the walls. You saw how she was when she got close to the trim when we painted the cottages for you," Robin teased.

"Hey." Sara grinned. "Okay, that might be the truth. But I'll help where I can."

"You're all so busy. I can't ask you to do that."

"You didn't ask, we offered," Robin insisted.

"I bet we can talk Jay into helping, too, if he can get away from the kitchen."

"Like if he'd ever give the new assistant cook we hired more responsibility?" Lillian shook her head.

"Yes, just like that." A wide grin overtook Robin's face and she shrugged. "Though I'm not sure that's ever going to happen."

"If we can get the house painted this weekend, for sure I can have it finished by the wedding." Gary nodded his head decisively. "That's the one part I was worried about getting finished in time."

"Perfect. I'm going to set it all up. Saturday at nine in the morning." Sara grabbed Robin's hand. "Let's go tell Charlotte and make some phone calls."

The two women hurried away and Lil looked at Gary. "I hate for all of them to give up their weekend."

"Doesn't seem like they mind."

"I guess not." Lillian sat back, pleased that things were coming together and Magnolia House would soon be finished.

The only bad part about that? The time was quickly approaching where Gary's job would be finished, too. And once again she wondered, and then what?

She looked across the table as he concentrated on making a note on the pad of paper beside his plate. Always organizing, always making lists. He glanced up and caught her watching him and smiled.

She'd miss their nightly dinners, talking to him... and that smile. The one that made her heart flutter and her pulse race.

Soon, all of that would be over when he finished his job.

CHAPTER 21

Lillian looked around at the crowd at Magnolia House that weekend. Charlotte and Ben were chatting away and painting the front room. Gary was up on a ladder painting ceilings a bright, crisp white, covering up the dingy yellowed color. Robin and Sara were painting the kitchen with Robin in charge of cutting in around the cabinets and windows. Noah had claimed he would do the bathrooms and headed off to do both the downstairs and upstairs baths. She helped wherever she was needed, bringing more paint, moving drop cloths, and painting the window frames and sills.

Robin had brought along a speaker, and music spilled through the rooms along with laughter.

Her heart swelled with gratitude and love for these people she cared so deeply for. And Gary, though of course, she didn't care about him in the same way.

But she did care about Gary, didn't she? She frowned slightly. She *did* care about him.

When had that happened?

Or was she just now admitting that to herself?

Jay walked in carrying a large box and broke her thoughts. "I thought I'd bring lunch over."

Robin turned and smiled at him. Lillian didn't miss the special smile Jay gave Robin in return.

"I'm famished. You're just in time." Sara put down her paintbrush and called out to the others. "Hey, Jay brought food. Come and get it."

Everyone poured into the kitchen and grabbed sandwiches and sodas, then piled out on the deck and sat on chairs and the long bench Gary had built along the railing.

"Looks like we'll have most of the painting finished today with all the help you've gotten." Gary sat beside her on the bench with Lucky at his feet. "I should be able to finish up what's left."

"I'm so grateful to all of them for the help."

"You've got a lot of great friends." An easy smile played at the corners of his mouth.

"I do. I'm very lucky."

Lucky looked up at her and wagged his tail at hearing the word lucky. She and Gary laughed.

"Look, he knows his name," Gary said. He reached down and petted the dog.

Everyone finished their lunch and then went back to work. By five or so everyone had headed out and she sat outside with Gary sipping sweet tea, glad to be off her feet.

"That was a long day." She let out a long sigh and kicked off her shoes.

"We got a lot of work done."

"That we did." She took a sip of her drink. "Are you hungry? We could go to the inn for dinner."

"There are some left-over sandwiches from all the food Jay brought. I think I'll just grab one of those in a bit. I want to get some more work done this evening."

Disappointment flitted through her that he'd turned her down, but that was silly because she'd spent the whole day with him. She finished her tea and stood. "I should head home and let you get back to work then."

He stood and took her glass. She grabbed her shoes. "I'll see you tomorrow?"

He nodded. She turned and headed down the stairs to the beach, not wanting to leave but not wanting to keep him from his work. She turned for one last look and he stood on the deck with Lucky right by his side. He waved, and she turned and headed back to the inn. She should probably help with the dinner rush anyway, though what she truly wanted to do was spend all the time she could with Gary before he finished the job.

CHARLOTTE AND BEN headed to the Lady Belle after leaving Magnolia House. They climbed aboard and Ben opened a bottle of wine. She sliced up cheese and apples and they went outside to sit and enjoy the evening breeze. They sat on the seats on the stern and she propped her feet up, glad to finally be sitting down.

A marina worker came hurrying up to the

boat. "Ben? You got a minute? We have a mess-up on an order. The customer is here and angry. He wants to speak to you."

Ben sighed and rose. "I'll be back." He climbed off the boat.

She sat and sipped her wine for a while until she got a bit chilled. She wandered inside to Ben's cabin and opened his drawers in search of a sweater to wear. She rooted around in the top drawer and took out a gray sweater and shrugged it on. As she started to close the drawer, a small gold box caught her eye. She reached for it and opened it. A gasp wrenched from her lips. A sparkly diamond set in a simple gold setting rested in the box.

"What are you doing?" Ben's voice caused her to whirl around.

She stood there holding the ring box while guilt swirled through her. "I—I was cold. I came in here to borrow one of your sweaters. I didn't mean—I—"

He stepped into the cabin and took the ring box from her. "Well, this sure isn't the way I planned it." A rueful look crossed his face. "I got this a while ago, but I was going to wait and ask you after Sara and Noah's wedding. So it would be more special or not take away from either your engagement or Sara's wedding. I mean if I had asked you and if you'd said yes."

Her heart pounded in her chest so hard she could barely move and she semi-realized she was holding her breath.

"But now that you found the ring…" He dropped to one knee. "Charlotte Duncan. I love you. I want to spend the rest of my life with you. Will you marry me?"

She didn't even pause. "Yes. Yes, I'll marry you." Tears trailed down her cheeks.

He stood and slipped the ring on her finger and took her into his arms, holding her close. "I do love you, Charlotte."

"And I love you, Ben Hallet."

He kissed her gently then laughed. "This was definitely not how I'd planned to ask you. I had this whole romantic day planned so it would be really special."

"But I ruined it by finding the ring."

"You didn't ruin anything." He hugged her. "You said yes. That's all I wanted."

"And you asked me to marry you. That's all I wanted." She wrapped her arms around him and rested her head against his chest. His heart beat in rhythm with her own, connecting them as if they were two parts of one being. His hand slowly trailed up her back, and she basked in the perfect moment.

CHAPTER 22

The next evening Gary got cleaned up and dressed into nicer shorts and a collared shirt. Lillian had finally insisted on making good on her offer of a home-cooked meal. He didn't know how she'd made the time to do it, but he was all for home cooking. Not that Jay's meals at the dining room weren't great. But it would be nice to be alone with Lillian instead of in a room filled with diners. She'd also promised they wouldn't talk work the whole time.

He sat down at the table and quickly checked his email. A brief message from Mel said he was making some progress and might have found a clue to where Brian had gone. That was good news. He hoped this lead panned out. He shut the laptop and stood.

His phone rang and he quickly answered it.

"Dad, hey, how are you?"

"Mason, good to hear from you. Everything going okay back there in Seattle?"

"Yes… but I wanted to let you know that the insurance company settled. A large settlement."

"Good, it was the right thing to do."

"Our liability premiums are going to shoot through the roof."

"Can't be helped at this point."

"Oh, Dad, that's Gelco company on my other line. Gotta get it. Just wanted to let you know about the settlement."

The line went dead and he clicked off the phone and sighed. He was glad the insurance company had settled for a large amount, though it did little to assuage his guilt.

Lucky looked up from where he was resting near the doorway and came over to him as if the dog could sense his unrest. He leaned down and petted him. He'd taken the dog to the vet this morning and no chip had been found. He'd bought the dog a collar and tag with Lucky engraved on it. After debating, he'd added his own cellphone number, not that he really considered Lucky *his* dog.

Suddenly he needed to get out of here and

into the fresh air. He'd just walk slowly so he wasn't too early. "Lucky, you want to go see Lillian?" The dog walked to the door, wagging his tail. "I guess that's a yes."

They headed over to The Nest and Lucky trotted up the deck stairs as if he owned the place.

"Lillian, you here?" he called through the screen door.

"Come on in."

He and Lucky found her in the kitchen. Her face was flushed—adorably so—and she had on a teal apron covering her simple sundress. Her feet were bare, of course. He'd noticed she took every opportunity to have bare feet. She looked so at home and relaxed in her kitchen.

"Smells good."

"Chicken dish, green beans simmered for hours in onion and bacon, and homemade bread. I love to make bread. Don't know why I don't do it more often. Oh, and a pie. Peach."

"That all sounds fabulous."

"It needs about thirty more minutes. Want to go sit outside? I made some sweet tea if you'd like some."

"That sounds good."

He followed her outside, and they sat on the

loveseat. Lucky roamed around the deck until he settled at their feet.

"I hope cooking this meal didn't cut into your day too much. I know your days are busy."

"They are, but this was a welcome break. I sometimes forget how much joy cooking brings me. But I did squeeze in some work at the kitchen table while the pie was baking."

"I finished up the plumbing repairs in the downstairs bath today. New faucet and it no longer drips."

"Glad you got it finished." She tilted her head. "But we're not going to talk business all night, remember?"

He laughed. "I remember. So what do you want to talk about?"

"I see Lucky has a collar and tag now. So he's officially yours?"

"No, not officially, but he didn't have a chip. Someone might still claim him. I just… well, if he gets lost and can't find my house, it has my number on it so someone can call me." Though he realized he wouldn't be there much longer, and it wasn't *his* house.

The thought of leaving the island and leaving Lillian didn't thrill him any. He'd gotten used to his life here on Belle Island. Enjoyed working with his hands. Enjoyed his nightly dinners with Lillian.

And it seemed easier to hide from his past here than in Seattle…

"You got quiet. What are you thinking about?" Lillian interrupted his thoughts.

"I—" He wasn't going to tell her about Seattle and the mess he left there, that's for sure. He settled on, "About how much I like the island. And this job. And…" He took a deep breath. "And how much I really enjoy spending time with you, Lillian Charm."

Her eyes widened in surprise at his candor. "I enjoy our time together, too."

He turned sideways in the seat and reached out and touched her jaw, trailing his finger along it, then cradling her face in his hand. She pressed her hand against his. He leaned close, so close he could feel her breath. Her eyes closed and with one last battle against any of his hesitation, he kissed her.

A gentle kiss, tentative. She kissed him back, her hands coming to rest on his shoulders. He deepened the kiss, then slowly pulled back.

A sigh escaped her lips and a smile spread across his face at the sound.

"That was… nice." And the totally-in-charge, self-confident woman looked at him almost shyly.

"It was. It was *very* nice."

He sat back and took her hand in his, enjoying the smooth feel of her skin against the rough skin of his own. She leaned close against him and they sat silently watching the waves.

ALL THROUGH DINNER Lillian had to concentrate on their conversation. Concentrate on his words. Concentrate on eating, one bite at a time.

Her thoughts kept floating back to the kiss. The very nice kiss. The unexpected kiss.

Though had she expected it? Her cheeks flushed at the memory of it...

... and the thought she wanted another one.

"This pie is delicious." Gary's words interrupted her thoughts of the kiss and hopes for another one.

"Thank you."

"How about I help you clear the dishes and if it's not too late, we'll go sit outside for a bit?" Gary asked.

"That would be nice."

Very nice. Maybe he'd kiss her again.

They cleared up the dishes and headed outside. Lucky looked up from where he was dozing by the railing, then closed his eyes again.

Gary turned her slowly to him and took her in his arms, pulling her close. "You are the best thing to happen to me in a long time," he whispered in her ear.

He placed a finger under her chin and tilted her face up to his, then kissed her again, exactly what she wanted. Her heart pounded in her chest and she clutched at his shirt as he pulled her even closer. He finally let her go and she wanted to demand he kiss her again. He must have read her mind because he *did* kiss her again. Then once more.

Contentment mixed with a restlessness flowed through her. A very strange combination.

He finally let out a little laugh. "We should go sit down... or I'll just stand here all night kissing you."

"And that would be a bad thing, why?"

A glint of deep longing settled in his coppery-brown eyes. And he kissed her again.

CHAPTER 23

Gary woke up early the next day and couldn't put his finger on why he felt so off-kilter. Last night had been wonderful. He must have kissed Lillian a hundred times. Or a million. But still not enough.

He padded into the kitchen and found Lucky sitting by his empty water bowl, giving him a look of disbelief. "Sorry, pup. I'll fill it now." He filled the water bowl, then the food bowl, then started his coffee.

He took a cup to the table and flipped open his laptop. The date stared back at him.

That's why he felt so off today. It was Dale's birthday. A day he'd sworn he'd never forget. He raked his hand through his hair, then buried his face in his hands, letting the pain wash over him in waves.

Crashing over him.

Drowning him.

He didn't deserve to have this newfound happiness with Lillian. He didn't. Not after what had happened to Dale.

He opened his browser and clicked on the news. Then sat his mug down on the table with a clatter, splashing droplets of coffee across the surface.

There it was. Right there in print. In an ugly coincidence since it was Dale's birthday today. The story had been revived in the national news and his picture was right there for everyone to see. Probably someone had gotten wind of the insurance settlement and stirred up the story yet again. He shut the laptop with a bit too much force and closed his eyes.

It would only be a matter of time before everyone knew who he really was.

A monster.

A killer.

It didn't matter that a court case had said he was innocent. It was his responsibility. It was all his fault.

He stood up slowly and sucked in air, but it

didn't seem to fill his lungs. A heaviness pressed down on him, smothering him, imprisoning him.

He told himself that he should get dressed and go find Lillian. It was better that she heard it from him than from someone else. But still, he just stood, not moving, unable to struggle through the pain.

LIL STOOD on the deck of The Nest, sipping her coffee early the next morning. The sky was tinged with pink from the sunrise. She spied Ruby and Mischief walking by on the beach and waved.

Ruby came up to the deck. "Good morning. I see you're out to catch the sunrise, too."

"Where are David and May?"

"I left them sleeping in bed, with May curled up almost on top of David. I swear that dog has to be attached to the man all the time."

"Would you like a cup of coffee?" Lillian raised her mug.

"Love one."

Ruby came up on the deck and Lillian brought her a cup of steaming coffee. They settled onto two chairs, watching the sky brighten.

"How did your dinner turn out last night? Did Gary enjoy your home cooking?"

"I think so." Lillian felt the heat of a blush cross her face at thoughts of all the kisses last night.

Ruby cocked her head and raised an eyebrow. "And… What's that look about?"

A smile spread across her face. "He… It was a magical night. The stars were out. Everything was perfect."

"And?"

"He kissed me."

"Ah, ha. I knew it. I could tell by your face." Ruby nodded vigorously. "So, do you like him?"

"I—" She paused and her forehead creased. "I—I do. He's wonderful to talk to. I really enjoy our time together. But it's silly to have feelings like this for someone I just met a few weeks ago, isn't it?"

"Some people fall in love at first sight."

"Oh, I don't love him. I just… I really, *really* like him." The warmth of another blush covered her cheeks.

"I'm happy for you. Love to see you doing something for *you*." Ruby shrugged. "You know, other than running the inn, which I know you love doing. But still, a person needs a well-rounded life. And a handsome man kissing you isn't all bad." Ruby's mouth curved in a teasing grin.

They finished their coffee and Ruby stood. "Come on, Mischief. We should head back and make David a big breakfast. I'm kind of hungry myself." She turned to Lillian. "I'll see you at The Yarn Society?"

"You will."

Ruby left and Lillian still sat outside thinking about last night. Suddenly she jumped up. She'd go see if Gary was eating breakfast in the dining room. If not, she'd bring him over some cinnamon rolls and enjoy a quiet breakfast with him. She was just keeping up her part of the bargain with him, of course. That meals were included in his pay for his work rehabbing the guest house.

That was all it was.

Not that she wanted another one of his kisses...

JAY SAT at the computer at the desk at the edge

of the kitchen. His eyes widened as he read the news on his screen. Their Gary Jones was none other than multi-millionaire Garrett Jones, head of GJ Industries. The company known for building hotels across the country along with office buildings and shopping malls.

"What are you looking at?" Robin walked up behind him, startling him.

He looked up at her. "Look at this." He pointed to the picture of Gary—Garrett. "It says he's the man responsible for the collapse of a hotel being built in Seattle where a man was killed. The insurance company just settled."

She looked over, resting her hand on his shoulder. Heat seared through him at her touch. He ignored it though. Ignored it completely.

"That is Gary, isn't it?" She leaned even closer, leaving only a fraction of space between them and continued reading the story. "It says inferior materials were used in the construction and the company covered up their use of them."

"Looks like they had a trial and there wasn't enough evidence to convict Gary." Jay sighed. "And we have a man like that fixing Magnolia House."

"We need to tell Lil." Robin frowned.

"Yes, we do. And I need to double-check everything this man has done."

"But why would a multi-millionaire be here on the island, posing as a carpenter fix-it guy? And Lillian is just paying him a fair wage, nothing special."

"I doubt he needs the money," Jay said wryly. "And my best guess is he's here hiding out. Using an alias so people wouldn't find out who he really is."

"I'll go find Lil right now. This is the last thing she needs. And I think she's started caring about him, too. But he's just been one big lie." Her voice held a tone of concern. She turned and left, leaving that empty feeling to the kitchen, yet again.

Jay got up from the computer with guilt rushing through him. He'd assured Lillian that he thought Gary was doing good work for her. But what if he was cutting corners and using sub-par material on Magnolia House too?

CHAPTER 24

Gary stood out on the deck with Lucky by his side. He should be working, yet he just stood and stared out at the waves, unmotivated to do anything. Lillian approached from the beach and he sucked in a long, deep breath for courage. Now was as good a time to tell her as any. Then he'd see that look in her eyes that he'd become so familiar with. The judgment. And sometimes pity. And sometimes anger.

She held a box in her hands. Probably bringing his breakfast. If only he could freeze time. Have a nice breakfast with her. Kiss her one more time before he told her the truth.

Maybe he could delay telling her for that long…

She took a step up the stairs and frowned, juggling the box to one hand as she reached for the stair railing with the other. Then he watched in horror as the whole staircase began to sway.

Her eyes widened with fear, and he told his feet to move. Get over there. Something wasn't right.

The stairs began to crumble beneath her. "Lillian." He screamed her name.

As if in slow motion as he tried to reach her, the box she was carrying dropped and flung cinnamon rolls around her. She grabbed the railing and swung off to the side, crashing to the sand. She cried out in pain as a long board fell across her legs.

Again.

It was happening again.

His body finally listened to his commands, and he swung down from the deck, dropping to the sand. "Lillian. Lil, are you okay?" He lifted the board from across her legs, his breath shallow, his heart pounding.

Her eyes were closed, but she opened them slowly. "I… I think I am." She started to sit up.

He pushed her back gently. "No, don't get up. That was quite a fall."

"I'm okay." But her look didn't convince him.

"I'm calling 9-1-1."

"No, that's silly. Just give me a moment."

He held his phone in one hand, debating. She'd fallen a good five or six feet. Hard.

"I think I'm okay. Really. Help me sit up."

"I still think I should call 9-1-1."

"If you don't help me, I'll just do it myself." Her no-nonsense look convinced him.

He gently put an arm around her and helped her sit.

"I think I'm okay."

"You keep saying that, but you have blood all over your leg." He frowned.

"Help me stand and we'll check it out. Probably cut it on the board."

"I don't understand. Those stairs were solid. More than solid." He glanced at the pile of jumbled boards. He'd built them to spec. More than spec. What had he done wrong?

"Help me up."

He helped her stand, and she stood there for a moment, trembling as he kept his arm firmly but gently around her.

"I'm bringing you inside." He wrapped an arm around her and she took a few weak steps forward. "I'm going to carry you. Don't argue with me." He swept her up in his arms and carried her inside and set her gingerly on the couch.

She leaned back against it, her face a bit pale.

"You should call your niece. Or 9-1-1."

"No, I don't want to bother her and I don't need 9-1-1."

"Call your niece or I will." He stood there staring at her with what he hoped was a look that deterred any further argument.

She pulled out her phone and showed him a smashed screen. "Don't think I'll be using this."

"I'll call over to the inn." He grabbed his phone and called the inn. "I need to speak to Sara. This is Gary Jones. Is she around?"

"Gary, it's Robin." Her voice sounded oddly cold, not its usual friendly, welcoming tone. "I haven't seen Sara this morning."

"I need to find her. Lillian's been hurt. She's here at Magnolia House."

Silence thundered through the phone for a brief moment. "I'll find her right now."

He turned to Lillian. "Are you sure I shouldn't call 9-1-1?"

"Positive, and quit asking." She pinned him

with a determined look. "And don't let Sara call either."

He knelt before her, examining the cuts on her leg. "That was an impressive leap away from the collapsing stairs."

She gave him a weak smile. "Instinct. I'm kind of impressed I got so far away from them, too."

"What can I do?" He wanted to turn back time. Make this all go away. But then he'd had that exact same thought so many times over the last year or so.

"Do you think you could get me a glass of water?"

"Of course." He hurried to the sink and grabbed her a glass. His hands shook and he forced himself to steady them. He glanced and saw Lucky standing on the other side of the door to the deck with an accusing look on his face. He let Lucky inside and the dog immediately walked over to Lillian and sat next to her, staring at her, as if checking on her.

She sipped the water and Gary knelt before her. "Are you *sure* you're okay? You still really do need to go get checked out."

"Aunt Lil." Sara and Robin came bursting through the door, followed by Jay who had nothing less than a murderous look etched on his features.

LILLIAN COULD SEE the fear in Sara's eyes and rushed to reassure her. "I'm okay. Just a little fall."

"It wasn't a *little* fall," Gary contradicted her as he stood, making way for Sara. "The stairs collapsed under her."

Sara dropped to the floor in front of her. "You *are* hurt. There's blood. Do you think you re-injured your hip?"

Jay knelt beside Sara. "You look pale."

Robin hovered close. "We should call 9-1-1 with a fall like that."

"No, you shouldn't. I'm fine." She heard the bit of a tremble in her voice and it annoyed her. "Really." *There, that sounded stronger.*

Jay stood and faced Gary. "The stairs collapsed? How the heck did that happen?" Anger and accusation were plain on his face. "Again? Did you cut corners on the materials *again*? And pocketed the difference like before? You're lucky you didn't kill someone yet again."

Gary's face turned ashen.

"Jay, what are you talking about?" She looked from Jay to Gary and back to Jay.

"This man is *Garrett* Jones. He's the CEO of GJ Industries. They used shoddy building materials and a hotel they were building collapsed and killed a worker."

Gary stepped forward, his eyes pleading. "Lil, let me explain."

"Not now." Jay cut him off with a wave of his hand. "We're taking Lillian to Dr. Harden and getting her checked out."

"Can you stand?" Sara asked.

"Of course." She wasn't exactly *sure* she could, and what was going on between Jay and Gary? Gary reached out to help her to her feet, but Jay shouldered him aside.

Jay helped her up, and she stood unsteadily. She grabbed onto his arm and Sara took her other arm. Jay started to lead her out the door. He paused and turned back to Gary. "You're fired. And I'll deal with you later."

CHAPTER 25

Gary walked out onto the deck, his hands trembling. Guilt rushed over him, in wave after wave. How could this have happened again? Lillian could have been hurt worse... or killed.

Just like Dale.

And now he couldn't blame it on Brian. This was all his fault.

He had no place in the building business any longer. He'd thought he'd done such a superb job with the repairs he was doing here. He'd obviously missed something, messed something up. Maybe it had been too long since he'd done hands-on carpentry.

Lucky sat by his side, looking up at him. It

almost looked like the dog had an accusing look on his face, too. Great. Just great.

He raked his hand through his hair. Jay had fired him, and he was sure Lillian would stand by his decision. Jay would tell her all the details of what had happened back in Seattle. How Dale had died.

It didn't matter that it was Brian who'd cut corners and bought inferior building supplies, pocketing the difference. *He'd* been the one to hire Brian, an old college buddy. Then he'd gotten too busy to double-check everything like he usually did, or maybe he would have found the discrepancies. Or maybe he would have listened to Mason when he'd mentioned he thought something was off on the accounts on the hotel they were building.

But he'd defended Brian, never dreaming his friend would do something like this. But Brian had and pocketed over a million dollars then disappeared after the collapse of the building.

He scrubbed a hand over his face, trying to get the picture of Dale and his family—he had two little girls and a lovely wife—scrubbed from his memory.

The truth was, he was the top man at the company—or had been. It was his final responsibility. It didn't matter that a jury had acquitted him. He was guilty. It was his company, his hire, his friend.

He turned and looked at the house. He was fired. The house wouldn't be finished in time if he left. But Jay had made it perfectly clear.

Fired.

He trudged inside. The least he could do was make a list of what still needed to be finished for whoever took over the job. It was mostly odds and ends. Some painting. He'd gotten the major work finished. Though they'd probably hire someone to go over all the work he'd done, and he didn't blame them.

Lucky sat by his feet while he worked on the list. He wanted to call and check on Lillian, but he had no one to call, really. No one would talk to him, he was sure.

But the town would talk. Surely he'd hear something if he stuck around a few days. Or he could hang out from a distance and see if he could catch a glimpse of Lil.

No, what he needed to do was *talk* to Lillian. She deserved that much. Explain about Seattle and apologize for what had happened to her here. Then, he would resign from his position with GJ Industries, no longer be on a leave of absence, he'd be… retired. Turn it over permanently to Mason.

He'd lost everything because of his decisions. And now he'd lost Lillian. Pain squeezed his heart, though he was used to the pain. Used to the inability to change the past.

Used to the guilt.

He looked down at Lucky. "What do you say? Want to find a new place to stay for a few days? I have to talk to Lillian. Then I'm leaving this town. Leaving her in peace."

And *then* what was he going to do with his life?

DR. HARDEN BRISKLY entered the exam room. "Lillian, what happened?"

"Ashley, I'm fine. There was a little accident at the house I'm having rehabbed." Lillian assured the doctor, thinking that everyone was just making a big fuss over her.

"It was *not* a little accident. The stairs collapsed, and she took a hard fall." Sara glared at her. Her niece had insisted on coming into the exam room with her while Robin and Jay insisted on sticking around in the waiting room. "She needs to be totally checked out. And what about her hip? What if she re-injured it?"

"Sara, let Ashley do her job."

Ashley checked her out and even did x-rays, though Lillian protested she didn't need them. Thankfully, nothing was broken. After cleaning and bandaging her legs, Ashley sent her home with admonitions to take it easy for a few days.

Jay helped her inside The Nest, though she protested she didn't need help. *Not that anyone was listening to her.*

Okay, she was a *bit* unsteady, but that was to be expected. She settled into her favorite recliner.

"I'll let you get some rest." Jay started to leave.

"Wait right there. You tell me what's going on with Gary."

Jay paused. Ah, someone was *finally* listening.

"Aunt Lil, why don't you rest for a while. Then we'll sort all this out."

"Don't treat me like an invalid or some little old lady. I'm neither. Jay, sit and tell me everything."

Jay perched on the edge of the couch and

Robin sat beside him. Sara, annoyingly, hovered near the recliner.

"Gary Jones is actually a multi-millionaire CEO of GJ Industries. Garrett Jones. His company was involved in buying sub-par building materials and pocketing the money. A building collapsed, and a man died. There was just a huge insurance settlement for the man's family. Though, you know how that goes. Big companies always seem to appeal decisions like that." Jay's eyes flashed in anger. "Now, in spite of all his assurances that he knew what he was doing, the stairs collapsed. Maybe he bought subpar material for the rehab and pocketed the difference."

"There's no way for him to do that. He buys the material from the hardware store on my account." She shook her head and tried to process everything Jay was saying.

"We should check all those receipts. Make sure he isn't buying things for himself." Robin frowned.

"I have checked the receipts. I know I can't know exactly how many boards or feet of wiring he's used, but nothing is out of line." Lillian turned to Sara. "Go sit down. You're making me nervous hovering like that."

Sara reluctantly sat on a chair across from her. "I think we should have Jay check over all the work Gary has done."

"I'm going to. As soon as I leave here."

"And, Aunt Lil. No more dates with Gary. He's lied to you. He's responsible for a man's death."

Lil tried to take it all in, but suddenly she was tired. Very tired. Too tired to argue with any of them. Gary just didn't seem like the type of person to cut corners. He was so exacting and particular. He also didn't seem like the kind of person to cheat his company out of millions of dollars to pad his own pockets. It just didn't make sense.

"I think I will rest for a little bit. Why don't you all go back to work?"

"I'm going to stay here with you," Sara insisted.

"No, you're going to work and I'm going to just sit here and knit or maybe nap." She pinned Sara with a stern look.

"Okay, but we'll check on you later," Robin said.

The three of them finally left, and she reached for her favorite teal throw and placed it over her lap. She eyed her knitting bag but didn't have the energy to even pick it up and work on the lace shawl she was making for Sara as a surprise for her for the wedding.

She closed her eyes, but images of the stairs collapsing beneath her raced through her mind.

And all those things Jay had said about Gary. Were they true?

She sighed and pulled the wrap tightly around her, suddenly chilled. It appeared Gary wasn't quite the man she thought he was. Maybe her instincts hadn't been so good after all.

CHAPTER 26

Gary had hung around The Nest last night, at a distance, hoping to catch Lillian alone. But Sara, Robin, and Charlotte had been there with her most of the evening. Then when Robin and Charlotte left, he could still see Sara sitting outside on the deck. He and Lucky had headed back to the small cottage he'd rented nearby on the beach.

This morning he once again hung out on the beach near The Nest. He saw Lillian come out on the deck with her coffee, limping a bit, which made him scowl. He gathered his courage and headed toward The Nest.

He climbed the stairs—which didn't collapse under him like his faulty stairway—and stood on the top step. "Lillian."

She turned toward him, but he couldn't quite read her expression. Not her usual welcoming smile, that much he was certain of.

"Can I talk to you for a moment? Then I'll leave you alone. I promise." He took a step forward.

She nodded, still not saying a word.

He crossed over to where she was sitting and leaned against the railing across from her. "How are you feeling?"

"I'm feeling a bit sore, but fine. And I wish everyone would quit fussing over me."

"First off, I want to apologize. For not telling you my name. Well, Gary has been a nickname that my family has called me ever since I was a boy. But I should have told you about Garrett Jones. What I did. What happened."

She looked at him, her brown eyes filled with unanswered questions. Accusation. And maybe a little judgment.

He sighed. "I can tell you the whole story. About how I hired my college buddy, Brian, and how he was in charge of the purchasing. He bought inferior materials and kept the million he saved. He did a good job of covering it up." The guilt crashed over him as it always did. "But I was the boss. I should have been on top of things and never let this happen."

Lil sat in silence, watching him.

He turned and looked out at the calm ocean, so in contrast to the steel-hard tension in his body. He turned back to her. "Dale, one of my workers, a foreman, was killed in the collapse. He was a fine man. Been with me over twenty years. Had two little girls and a wife who loved him very much." He shuddered and closed his eyes briefly. "It should never have happened. I blame myself as much as Brian. I should have known something was off on the accounts. My son, Mason, asked me to check into it. I actually had the paperwork on my desk to look at, but I was just so busy. Which is really no excuse."

"And the article in the paper said the insurance company settled with Dale's family?" Her voice was low. "Is your company going to try and fight that?"

"What?" He looked at her in surprise. "No, I was the one who insisted they settle and give a large settlement. It was my company's fault. Dale's family deserves all the money they can get. Though, that won't bring back Dale, will it?"

"No, it won't." She sat there staring at him.

More than anything, right at this moment, he wanted to be anyone but himself. He wanted to go back to being just Gary Jones, the carpenter, the repairman. Though, he wasn't much of a carpenter either. He could have killed Lillian with his faulty staircase.

"Anyway, I wanted to come and say I'm sorry. Explain why I used my nickname. I just needed some time out of the spotlight. Some time to regroup. Mason took over running the company. I've been teaching him for years. I hope he'll do a better job at the helm than I did." He shrugged. "The board of directors asked me to step down for a bit, but I've decided to permanently quit as the CEO. I'll turn that over permanently to Mason."

"Why?"

"Because I can't even build a simple set of stairs. I thought I still remembered everything I learned about carpentry. Obviously I didn't. I'm so, so sorry about the collapse and so thankful you weren't hurt worse." The guilt was almost impossible now, like a building collapsing on him. Smothering him. Crushing him.

"I don't think what Brian did was actually

your fault." Lillian looked directly at him and he saw no judgment in her eyes.

"Ah, but you see. It was. I hired him. He was my friend. I just let him have at the purchasing and didn't watch over him like I would have with any other hire."

"So your fault, what you're guilty of, was trusting a friend?" She eyed him.

"It was misplaced trust."

She nodded. "It appears it was."

"Anyway, I'm sorry about everything. Hiding my past, and especially for not making the stairs correctly. I keep going over in my mind what I did wrong, but I can't figure it out. It's all just a jumble of boards now, so I guess I'll never know. Rest assured I won't be building anything, ever again."

She sat there, with the stark white bandages on her legs taunting him and nailing his guilt.

"I think you're very hard on yourself." Her words were spoken so softly he could barely catch them on the gentle breeze.

He pushed off the railing. "I'm sorry, Lil. Sorry for everything. I'm leaving the island now. I hope you can find someone who can finish the guest house for you. I'm sorry I didn't get it finished by the wedding. I wish you the best and hope the wedding is wonderful." He turned and headed back across the deck.

"Goodbye, Gary."

He turned back and took one last look at her sitting there in the sunshine. Her honey-brown eyes glistening with a hint of tears. "Goodbye, Lillian."

CHAPTER 27

J ay strode into The Lucky Duck late that afternoon. Ben, Noah, and Delbert were sitting at a table finishing up their lunch. He slid into a booth beside them.

"You look terrible." Ben stared at him.

"Rough couple of days."

"So I heard. But Lillian's okay?" Noah asked.

"The girls are with her now. They made her lunch. They're probably driving her crazy about now." Jay caught Willie's eye and ordered a beer.

"You're not going to eat?" Ben pushed away his completely empty plate.

"I grabbed something at the inn before I

came here." He reached for the beer the waitress brought and took a long swig.

"They were just telling me about Garrett Jones." Delbert reached for his beer. "I thought something was familiar about him when I met him. Just didn't tie the casually dressed Gary with the business suit Garrett. His company actually gave us bids on two Hamilton Hotels we built."

"Looks like you dodged a bullet on not using them." Jay set his glass down. "I should have checked the guy out more carefully. I should have never let Lillian hire him in the first place."

"Since when does anyone 'let' Lillian do anything?" Noah cocked his head. "Besides, when she got rid of Vince, she needed someone to finish the work."

"That reminds me." Ben crumbled his napkin and set it by his empty plate. "I heard rumors around town that Vince is bad-mouthing Lillian for firing him. Rumor has it that he's not getting many jobs at all now and he blames Lil."

"Of course he's not blaming himself for doing lousy work and rarely showing up to the job site." Jay shook his head.

"There's talk that he's going to get even with

her." Ben frowned. "But I'm not sure how he could do that."

Jay sat back, thinking. He rubbed his chin and stood up abruptly. "I've gotta go."

"You just got here. You've got half a beer left." Noah pointed to his glass.

"There's something I've got to do."

Jay hurried out into the sunshine. Things were starting to make sense. He'd gone over every inch of the work on the guest house yesterday and this morning. Nothing looked out of place. Gary did better work than he, himself, could do. Very precise and very well done. So he hadn't been able to figure out what went wrong on the stairs.

He strode down the sidewalk until he passed the inn and went around to the beach side of the guest house. He walked over to the lumber, piled this way and that, where the stairs used to be. He bent over and carefully studied the boards.

Then he saw it. A cut all the way through the riser of the stairs. He dug another riser out and saw another cut. He hardly had to sort through and find the third support riser. He knew what he'd find. Another cut.

Sure enough, he did. Then he looked

carefully at the support posts and found more cuts. Someone had sabotaged the stairs.

And he was *certain* he knew who it was.

LILLIAN INSISTED on going to The Yarn Society even though Sara wanted her to stay home and take it easy. How hard was it to go and sit with her friends and knit? Besides, if she sat here any longer feeling sorry for herself, she was going to scream.

Sara insisted on driving her to the community center despite her insistence that she was perfectly able to walk. Though, she did admit she was sore from the fall in places she didn't even know she had.

Dorothy and Ruby jumped up when she entered the room. "Lillian, we didn't think you'd be here today." Dorothy rushed over and hugged her. "I'm so glad you're okay. Ruby was just telling me about what happened."

No surprise her friends already heard the news.

"Sit down." Ruby led her over to a chair. "And Charlotte told me all about Gary. Or

Garrett. Or whatever he calls himself today. Are you okay?"

Lillian settled into a chair and took out her knitting. It was a good thing this wrap she was knitting for Sara was an easy to memorize pattern because her friends were not finished with their questions.

"You sure you're okay? I heard it was quite a fall." Dorothy sat down next to her and picked up her knitting, her needles starting to dance in a steady rhythm.

"I'm fine. Just sore."

"And I heard that Garrett's company was sued. Something about using inferior materials in the hotel they were building."

She told her friends what she knew about the whole episode. Then she told them about Gary coming over today and talking to her.

"So, he blames himself?" Ruby asked as she stopped her knitting. "He didn't actually buy the inferior material or cover it up."

"But he's ultimately in charge. Just like if something goes wrong at Charming Inn. Ultimately, it's my responsibility."

"Maybe, but a person can let guilt over someone else's mistake—or outright deceit—eat at them until it ruins their life. It seems a shame for Gary to let this ruin his." Ruby started knitting again. "Besides, you like him, don't you? Does this change anything?"

"He didn't tell me the truth about who he really was." Lillian frowned. "And really, I only met him a few weeks ago, so I guess I don't really know him that well, do I?"

"I think you can learn a lot about a person in a short time. Who they really are. Even if you don't know everything about their past." Ruby sighed. "Look at David and me. I met him and he hid the fact he'd had cancer. But it didn't matter to me. He's a good man and I love him. We'll face whatever the future brings." Ruby looked at Lillian closely. "Maybe you should figure out how you feel about him and if you want to give him another chance."

Lillian paused her knitting. Did she want to give him another chance? She didn't really know him that well anyway, did she? Wasn't it easier to just let it all go and get back to normal life?

As if Dorothy could read her thoughts, her friend said, "And don't just take the easy way out. Figure out what you really want."

CHAPTER 28

Gary opened the door to his rental cottage and his eyes widened in surprise. "Mason. What are you doing here?"

"Checking on you. I booked a flight after I saw the story about the collapse went national again. I looked for you at Charming Inn. Thought you were staying there. But some blonde gave me an earful about how you'd built a shoddy staircase and some Lillian woman had been hurt. What's that all about? You've never built anything that wasn't over-engineered and built to perfection."

"You mean except the hotel that collapsed."

Mason pushed past him, shaking his head, and strode into the cottage. His son stopped and stared at Lucky in amazement and turned back to him. "You have a dog?"

"Not really." He shrugged. "Well, I guess he is. He just kind of showed up at the house I was rehabbing and then stuck around. No one has claimed him."

Mason bent down and petted Lucky. "How are you, boy?"

"His name is Lucky."

"Glad to meet you, Lucky." The dog wagged his tail and Mason stood back up. "What's this nonsense about the stairs collapsing?"

"They did. Right before my eyes. I must have messed up something on the understructure, though I keep running it through my mind and can't figure it out."

Mason shook his head. "I just don't see it. You wouldn't make a mistake like that."

He was pleased his son defended him, but the facts were there. He'd built the new stairs, and they'd fallen and Lil had been hurt.

"So who is this Lillian who got hurt?"

"She owns Charming Inn. And hired me to rehab the guest house. I was actually really enjoying it. And Lillian and I became friends." He led Mason over to the fridge, grabbed two beers, and handed one to his son. "But then she found out about who I really was and… well, things fell apart."

"How long are you going to keep blaming yourself for what happened at the hotel? It was Brian's fault. The jerk got away with around a million bucks and disappeared. It's *his* fault." Mason looked at him. "And don't give me the whole I'm the boss lecture. Yes, you were. And we've put new procedures in place so it can never happen again. But you weren't the one who actually caused the collapse."

"I'm still responsible. The buck stops here."

"All I can see is the guilt stops here." Mason eyed him. "Why don't you come back to Seattle. It's time you took back over the role of CEO."

"No, I'm going to resign. Permanently."

"You can't do that." Mason took a step forward. "I'm not ready to be the permanent CEO. I was iffy about taking it on temporarily."

"And you think the board of directors wants me back?" He eyed Mason skeptically.

"I know they do. They weren't pleased when the story broke again, but it will blow over soon."

"I don't know…" He wasn't sure about anything anymore, much less making a big decision like this. "I need time to think."

"Sure, I'll give you a couple of days. But I'm staying here with you. You got room? I need your help on some things." Mason nodded to his laptop bag.

"I'll help you now, but I'm not sure about resuming CEO responsibilities."

"It looks like I'll have a few days to convince you."

"How did you find me here, anyway?"

"Small town, Dad. I asked around at a few places and someone at The Sweet Shoppe said you'd rented this place. Gotta love small towns. And have you ever had one of the almond scones at The Sweet Shoppe? They're great." Mason grinned at him.

"Glad you're here, son."

Jay met Lillian at the front door of the inn when Dorothy dropped her off after The Yarn Society meeting. She made sure her knitting was securely tucked away in her bag so Sara didn't spy it. Sara was sure to be lurking around here somewhere, waiting to check on her yet again.

"Lil, I need to talk to you." He took her arm

and led her over to a corner where they could have some privacy.

"If you want to talk about Gary—Garrett— I don't really want to hear any more."

"No, this isn't about Gary. Well, it is, but this is different."

She let out a sigh and sank onto the overstuffed chair at the edge of the lobby. "What is it?"

"The stairs collapsing? That wasn't Gary's fault."

She looked at Jay in surprise. "It wasn't? But he built them."

"And someone sabotaged them. Made some cuts so that when someone put their weight on them, they'd fall."

"But who would do that? And why?"

Jay's eyes narrowed. "There's talk around town that Vince is mad you fired him. Thinks that's why he's not getting jobs. And he's made some threats against you."

"I can't believe he'd do that. I thought he was just lazy, not evil."

"I called the sheriff, and he's going to look into it."

"Did you tell Gary? Does he know it's not his fault?"

"He left the guest house. Maybe the island."

She stood. "I have to find him. I'll call around and see if anyone knows where he is. He came by this morning to talk to me, so he was still here then."

Jay looked surprised. "He did?"

"He apologized for not telling me about his past and for the stairs collapsing. But I don't think he owed me all the facts about his past, and now he needs to know it wasn't his fault that the stairs fell." She whirled around to go drop off her knitting at The Nest and start making calls. It was hard to stay hidden in a town like Belle Island. Surely someone knew where he was.

CHAPTER 29

For the second time that day, Gary was surprised when he opened his door. "Lillian."

"Gary, we need to talk." She brushed past him and walked inside, uninvited. She stopped when she saw Mason sitting at the table. "Oh, I'm sorry. You have company."

"Lillian, this is my son, Mason."

Mason rose and came over and shook Lillian's hand. "Good to meet you."

"It's good to meet you, too." Lillian stared at Mason, then turned to him. "You two look so much alike."

Mason laughed. "I hear that all the time. A mini-Garrett."

Gary looked from Mason to Lillian, unsure why she was here.

She stepped forward, standing right in front of him. "The stairs weren't your fault."

That was an abrupt change in conversation, but of course, they were his fault. "Lil—I built them."

"You did. But it looks like Vince sabotaged them."

His eyes flew open. "He what?"

"Jay found cuts in the supports. The sheriff is looking into it."

"Ha, I told you, Dad. You'd never, ever build steps that would fall. If anything, you'd have them over-supported." Mason walked over and snapped his laptop shut. "I'm going to get some fresh air. Take a walk on the beach. I'll leave you two alone to talk."

Gary stood holding onto the back of a chair, taking all this in. Vince had done this? Anger rushed through him. Lillian could have been hurt worse than she was. Why would he do that? He finally gathered his thoughts and his manners. "Lil, take a seat." He motioned to the couch.

She sat down and stretched out her legs. The ones with the bandages, but at least they weren't taunting him anymore. He took a seat in the chair across from her.

"I was with the Yarnies—my knitting friends —and we were talking. My friend Ruby is very wise. She said you can get to know a person in a very short time. I feel like I know you even though it's only been a few weeks. I know you feel guilty about Dale's death and that probably won't ever totally go away. But I think you need to find a way to forgive yourself. Know it wasn't you who caused the accident. I know you feel responsible because you run the company. But you can only do so much. You have to rely on the people you hire. And sometimes we make mistakes on who we hire. Like I did with Vince. Luckily his sabotage didn't result in someone getting killed. But it could have."

He took in the warmth in her eyes. There was not a hint of judgment in them and he felt the tiniest bit of guilt begin to ebb slowly away from the stranglehold it had on his heart.

She leaned forward and touched his face. "I… I care about you. I really enjoy spending time with you. I'd like to spend more time with you."

He covered her hand with his. A bolt of electricity ran through him. Through them.

His phone rang, and he wanted to ignore it, but maybe it was Mason. He glanced at it, leaned back and gave Lillian the just-a-minute sign, and stood, walking away into the kitchen.

Mel's voice came through the other end of the line. "I found him. Small island, actually not far from you. You can get to it by small plane or boat. I can send you all the info. Doesn't look like he's moving anywhere anytime soon. He's got a villa there on the beach."

"Okay, thank you. I'll take it from here."

He slipped the phone in his pocket and walked back over to Lillian. "I've got to go."

She looked up at him in surprise.

"I'm sorry. It can't wait." He did want to stay and work things out with Lillian, but not now. Not until he did this.

Lillian stood. "Okay. I just wanted you to know about the stairs." He could see the hurt in her eyes like she wanted something else from him—*needed* something else from him.

But he had something he had to do. To try to make things right.

MASON WALKED ALONG THE BEACH, enjoying the

sunshine. It had been raining for what seemed like weeks in Seattle. Cloudy, gray days. Day after day. But here the sun threw golden light around him and danced like diamonds on the gently rolling waves.

He walked toward Charming Inn, intrigued by the inn and the guest house and the inn's owner, Lillian. Who, if he wasn't mistaken, his father was rather taken with.

The blonde who had given him a piece of her mind when he'd gone into the inn looking for his father was standing on the beach, looking out at the waves. He considered turning around and heading back the way he came to avoid her.

Too late. She spied him and waved to him, heading briskly in his direction.

"Hey, I want to apologize," she said as she stood next to him. "I was out of line and I heard I was wrong, too. The stairs weren't your father's fault."

"No, they weren't. And neither was the collapse of the hotel we were building in Seattle." He defended his father.

"I know. I'm sorry. I just get overly defensive of Lillian. She means the world to me." The woman held out her hand. "Robin. Robin Baker."

He took her hand in his, surprised by the firmness of her handshake. "Mason Jones."

"And that's your full name, your real name?" She tossed him a teasing smile.

"It is." He grinned back at her, warming up to this woman he'd first thought was cold and aloof.

"So you came to visit your dad?"

"Actually I came to check up on him after that story broke again about the hotel collapse. I wish it would just… go away."

"I bet." She nodded in agreement.

"So, what's up between Lillian and my father?"

Robin pursed her lips and cocked her head to one side, letting her blonde hair spill across her shoulder and glisten in the sunlight. "I'm not sure. They've gone on a few dates. They're friends." She shrugged. "Or maybe more?"

"I think he has a thing for her. I can tell by the way he talks about her. And the way his eyes lit up when she came over today to the cottage my dad is renting."

"He's got a cottage here?"

"Just down the beach." He bent his head that direction then paused when his phone buzzed. "Geez, a guy can't even take a little beach walk."

She looked at him, puzzled.

"Just got a text from my dad. Said he's leaving right now and to stay at the cottage and he'll get back with me. That's cryptic." He frowned, confused himself. "I don't know what in the world would make him just take off like that."

He turned back to Robin. "So, it looks like I'm on my own for a bit and I know absolutely no one on the island." He glanced at her ring-bare fingers and took a chance. "Want to show me this island that my father is so enthralled with? I'll even buy you dinner."

She looked at him for a moment, glanced back at the inn, then turned back to him. "I'd love to."

CHAPTER 30

G ary watched out the window as the small seaplane dipped down to land on the water near a long pier at this out-of-the-way island somewhere in the Caribbean. Looks like his friend must have done very well with the money he stole. He took a deep breath, gathering his courage for the upcoming confrontation. He disembarked and told the pilot he'd be back soon. Perks of having enough money to hire a private plane.

And he hoped he'd be back soon. First, he had to find Brian. He punched in the address that Mel had given him and located the cottage where Mel said Brian was staying.

He got a taxi—it was the only one on the island—and headed out. He rode along a twisty road with brilliant views of the turquoise ocean. It was beautiful here. And Brian was living his life, no consequences for his actions, living off the millions he'd stolen. That ended today. He had the phone number of the local police, but first, he wanted to confront Brian, face-to-face.

Then he'd haul his sorry butt back to the states and have him prosecuted for murder.

He noticed a few small cottages—some he'd almost consider huts—scattered along the dirt road as they drove along. Not exactly the rich island paradise he'd been expecting. They got to the address and saw a battered jeep sitting in the drive. Hopefully that meant Brian was here. He handed the driver a twenty. "Wait for me. I won't be long."

He knocked on the door to the tiny cottage —much simpler and smaller than he'd imagined. When no one answered he walked around the side of the cottage. There on the beach was Brian... with a young girl and a woman he didn't know. Brian was in the shallow waves, tossing the girl into the air. Her laughter rang across the distance. The woman sat on a chair, filming them with her phone. The perfect family scene, though as far as he knew, his friend didn't have a family. But Dale had a family. One who missed him terribly now.

With doubled resolve, he steeled himself and crossed over to the beach. Brian put a hand up, shielding the sun from his eyes and watched him approach. He set the girl down, took her hand, and walked her up to the woman. He said something to her, and she turned to look at him. He saw the raw fear in her eyes.

She gathered up the girl in her arms and headed back to the cottage, passing by him on the beach. "Listen to him. Please. And I'm sorry how everything turned out. What happened." She glanced at the girl, clutching her tightly against her. With one more beseeching look, she went into the cottage.

Brian walked up to him. "Garrett. I can't say I'm surprised to see you here. I knew it was just a matter of time."

"You stole from me and your actions cost Dale his life. He has daughters and a wife that miss him." He stared at Brian. "How could you do that? I trusted you. I thought I knew you."

"I…" Brian turned and look out at the vast occan spreading before them. "I needed the money."

"You needed the money? What for? To buy

a place here on this island and enjoy your perfect life?" Anger flooded through him and he clenched his fists.

"No, the cottage is Ellie's—my wife's—not mine. Her grandfather gave it to her to live in."

"You're married?"

"I am now." He turned and looked at the cottage. "And that beautiful little girl? She's my daughter. I only found out a few years ago. Ellie looked me up when she needed help. We'd had a thing—a fling—when I was down in the Caribbean in St. Thomas for vacation. It was before I joined your company. Anyway, Ellie told me then that Addison—Addy—was my daughter."

"What does this have to do with you stealing almost a million dollars?"

"Addy was sick. She needed an operation— an experimental surgery that could save her life. No insurance would cover it and Ellie had no way to pay for it, so that's when she came to me. I tried borrowing money and put everything I owned up as collateral. But the medical bills climbed. So… I started messing with the books at GJ Industries. I bought inferior materials but covered it up. I got some kickbacks on other things I ordered. Anything to raise money."

"Why didn't you just ask me for money?"

"I couldn't do that. I'd already been cheating you. I thought it would be a onetime deal. But the bills kept coming. How could I then ask you for money?" Brian raked his hand through his hair, his eyes tortured with pain. "But I had no idea this would happen. I thought the building would be fine. Just not made to quite as high standards."

Gary turned and looked at the cottage and saw Ellie staring out the window at them. He turned back to Brian. "So you stole for Addy?"

"I did. Ellie would have sold this cottage if she'd owned it. But she doesn't. And her family doesn't have any money, either. I was desperate."

Gary stood there watching the raw pain slash across Brian's face.

"Then the building collapsed, and I knew I had to get out of there. Addy was having a difficult time with her recovery and it was touch and go. If I stayed and owned up, got arrested, I couldn't be here for Addy and…" He scrubbed a hand over his face. "She needed me. She still does. Her health is fragile, but that surgery gave her the only chance she had at life."

"I wish you'd come to me."

"I wish I'd done lots of things differently and I'll be haunted by Dale's death until my own last breath." Brian turned and stared at him. "I'm so sorry for the consequences of my actions. Though I'd do it all over again if I had to. I'd do anything to save Addy's life. Anything."

Gary stood there facing the stranger who had once been his friend. "I've thought so many things about you over the last few years. I've been so angry. Hurt. Furious. And mostly I've wondered how the man I thought I knew could do this. Steal the money." He turned and looked at the little girl standing at Ellie's side in the window. "But now, I can see why you did. At least understand a little bit. But it was still wrong."

"I know that. But… Addy is scheduled for another surgery next week." Brian looked at him, an imploring look in his eyes. "I need to be there with her. Be there for her."

Gary turned and looked out at the sea. Choices. There were always hard choices to be made in life. What would he have done to save Mason's life? Probably just about anything. Though hopefully not something that had such deadly consequences.

He turned back to Brian. "I'm heading back now. You go be with your daughter for her surgery."

"Really?" Brian's eyes filled with gratitude.

"I don't see what good it would do to have that little girl go through something so scary without her father at her side."

Brian reached out and clasped his hand. "I don't know what to say."

"Say that eventually you'll make this right. You'll come back and face the consequences. Come back when Addy is out of the woods. I'll help you in any way I can."

Brian shook his hand. "You have my word."

Gary turned around, hoping that Brian's word was as good as it used to be. He waved to the little girl in the window, and she gave him a shy smile.

He walked away, hoping that Addy's surgery was successful, and she'd live a long, happy life. But for now, this secret was his to keep, until Brian came back and faced the music.

CHAPTER 31

L il sat in her recliner, reading more entries in the journal, trying to keep her mind occupied. Gary had just jumped up and left earlier today. They'd been talking, and she'd basically put it out there that she didn't judge him for what happened back in Seattle. She'd said she cared for him and wanted to spend time with him.

And he'd gotten up and left. No explanation.

She was such a fool. It had only been a few weeks. She didn't know him at all.

… though she'd felt like she did.

She set the journal down. This was not the time to concentrate on it and figure things out.

She'd get back to it after Sara's wedding. After things settled down. After... she wasn't so hurt.

Her heart twisted in her chest as she got up to make a cup of hot tea. She'd taken a chance. She'd tried. Evidently Gary wasn't on the same level as she was. He'd been so eager to leave after he'd gotten that phone call. Fine. Go take care of whatever. Right when she'd placed her heart out there in the open for him.

She made the tea and sat back down. Then got up to adjust a picture that wasn't hanging straight on the wall. Then decided to fold her teal throw neatly and put it on the back of the couch. Then the magazines needed straightening.

Then she couldn't see anything else that needed to be fixed. Except maybe her heart.

MASON SAT WORKING LATE that night after spending a wonderful afternoon and evening with Robin. She was charming and funny and regaled him with stories of the town and its people. She'd even taken him out to Lighthouse Point and told him about the legend of making a wish, throwing a shell, and then your wish would come true.

Not that he believed that kind of nonsense.

He wondered if maybe he should ask her out again while he was here, though he only planned on staying a few days.

He looked up in surprise to see his father enter the cottage. He jumped up and crossed over to him. "You look beat. Where'd you go?"

"Had to… go settle something."

Still cryptic, but he didn't pry.

His father looked at his watch. "Took longer than I expected to get back here. It's later than I thought." He sighed. "I wanted to go see Lillian, but it will have to wait until tomorrow."

His dad walked to the fridge and grabbed a beer. "Want one?"

He nodded.

They sat down at the kitchen table and his dad stretched out his legs and scrubbed a hand over his face. "So much has happened in the last few days."

"So much has happened in the last few *weeks*. Like you masquerading as a mere carpenter. And then there's this Lillian thing."

"Yes, there is this *Lillian thing*. If only I knew what it was."

He stared at his dad, searching his face. Then his lips twitched into a smile. "Hey, you've fallen for her, haven't you?"

His dad rubbed his chin. "I do believe that I have. Don't care that it's only been a few short weeks."

Mason glanced at the date on his watch and did some quick math. "Three and a half weeks. Almost four since you left Seattle."

"Four weeks? That means Sara's wedding is this coming weekend, only five days from now."

"Sara? That friend of Robin's?"

"How do you know Robin?"

"I kind of hung out with her this afternoon." He grinned. "And evening. Took her to dinner at a place called Magic Cafe. Great food."

His dad frowned.

"What's wrong?"

"Nothing. I just kind of thought that she and Jay were dating."

"Who's Jay?"

"He's the chef at Charming Inn."

"She didn't say anything about dating anyone." Mason shrugged.

"I guess I was mistaken." His dad took another swallow of beer and stood. "I'm headed to bed. Long day. And I want to get up early and go find Lillian."

Mason leaned back and nursed his own beer as his dad headed down the hallway. He still wondered where his dad had disappeared to earlier. Then his thoughts bounced back to the great day he'd spent with Robin. Yes, he was going to call her tomorrow—he'd been smart enough to get her number—and ask her if she wanted to have dinner with him again.

CHAPTER 32

L illian sat outside the next morning, sipping her coffee, still feeling the sting of rejection after telling Gary how she felt. Just a silly old woman. What did she know about dating? She'd lived all these years without being married or even having a serious boyfriend. And her life had been full. She didn't need anything or anyone else.

She was *fine*. She'd just momentarily been thrown a bit off-kilter. She'd get over it. She always did. Life threw curves and she adjusted.

The last few days had been such a roller coaster. Finding out Gary wasn't who he'd implied he was. Learning what had happened in Seattle. Her fall from the stairway. Then... telling Gary she cared about him.

And he'd up and left.

She was ready for some stability. Some normal life. Well, as soon as they made it through Sara's wedding this weekend, only a few days away.

"Lil."

She turned at the sound of Gary's voice, annoyed that it made her heart do a double beat and her pulse race.

He climbed the stairs and came toward her, dropping in front of her so their eyes were level. "I'm so sorry I left so quickly yesterday."

She stayed stonily silent, unwilling to let her traitorous heart soften.

"I had something I had to take care of. I had to… make peace with something. The timing was lousy though. Because—"

She interrupted him. "No problem," she lied. "I hardly know you. And if you had somewhere to be, it's not any of my business."

"But it was a problem. I shouldn't have left like that, but I really needed to deal with something. I don't blame you if you don't forgive me for leaving like that." He looked right at her. "But I heard what you said. That you… care. Care about me."

She held her breath, waiting for his words.

Her heart, traitorous indeed, squeezed in her chest. Silly heart.

He took her hand in his. "I hated leaving because I wanted to tell *you* something. Tell you that these last few weeks have been the best weeks of my life. I care about you, too, and want to spend time with you. Lots of time. Like forever and ever time."

She sat there in shock, barely able to hear him over the pounding of her heart.

"You know how when I first came here and I offered to help with the guest house? Jay was unsure, but you said when the universe drops something in your lap, you say thanks and accept it? Well, the universe dropped something very, very special right in front of me when I came to this island." He squeezed her hands. "And I'd be a fool to let you go. I love you, Lillian Charm. I think I have since the second day I was here on the island. You saw me on the beach and we sat and talked. You were so excited about Sara's wedding. And we sat and watched the sunset. I felt so connected to you then."

She could hardly put her thoughts together as her heart swelled in her chest and happiness surged through her. "You love me?" She wanted to make sure she'd heard him correctly.

"I do."

"And that stuff about forever and ever?"

"Yes, I meant it. I want to spend forever with you."

"But I've lived alone all these years. I don't know if I'd even know how to share my life with a man. I'm…" She let out a little laugh. "I'm pretty set in my ways."

"I'll adjust." He smiled. "I don't have a ring to give you—yet. But I want to marry you. Be with you. I want you by my side. Share the rest of our lives."

"But it's only been four short weeks. What will people say? It's all so… fast."

"I don't care what people say or think. And it doesn't matter how long it's been. I know how I feel."

She reached out and touched his face. "And I know how I feel, too. I do love you. Truly I do. And I'd love to spend the rest of my life with you."

"Now, that's what I'm talking about." He jumped up and pulled her to her feet and into his arms. He kissed her gently then pulled back.

"Lillian Charm, we're going to have the most perfect life together."

"You know what? I believe you." She stood on tiptoe. "Now how about you kiss me again?"

And he did as she asked.

CHAPTER 33

Lillian stood in The Nest helping Sara get ready. Charlotte and Robin were due back in at any moment. They'd gone out to make sure everything was ready. "You look lovely. Your mother's dress turned out so fabulous on you."

Sara slowly ran her hands down the bodice of the dress. "I need to thank Ruby again. She did magic with the dress." She spun around in front of the mirror.

"I have a present for you." Lillian handed her a box wrapped in white paper with gold ribbon.

Sara carefully opened the present and gasped. "Oh, Aunt Lil. It's perfect." She wrapped the lace shawl around her shoulders. "So delicate and so beautiful." She hugged her.

"I thought you might want to wear it this evening if it gets chilly since we'll be outside for the reception."

"I have a present for you, too." Sara smiled and reached for a package beside her. "I had Ruby make it."

Lillian reached for the package. "It's not my wedding. What is it?"

"Open it and see."

Lillian opened the wrapped present and her eyes filled with tears. "Is this from Leah's dress?" She held up a lace clutch bag.

"It is. I talked to Ruby about making it for you. I wanted you to have a part of Mom's wedding dress, too."

"I love it." She clasped the bag close, feeling like her sister was looking down on both of them.

Robin and Charlotte entered the room. "Oh, you gave her the surprise." Robin clapped her hands.

"You knew about this?"

"Oops. Sort of. Maybe Sara mentioned it."

"Well, you did a good job keeping the secret."

"Guess what we just heard?" Charlotte walked over to Lil. "The sheriff found security video from the house next to Magnolia House. There's video of Vince tampering with the stairs. The sheriff arrested him today."

"Gary knows now, too. He looked… relieved," Robin added.

Charlotte walked over and spun Sara around. "I knew this dress would be perfect on you. You look gorgeous. Are you ready for this?"

"I've never been more ready for anything in my life. I feel like I've waited forever for this day."

"I couldn't be more happy for you." Lillian hugged her, then took her arm. "Let's go get you married to Noah."

Her niece rested her arm on hers, and they walked through the inn and down to the start of the aisle. Noah stood under the arbor with Zoe by his side.

Charlotte and Robin walked side by side down the aisle and turned and waited for Sara.

"You ready?" Lillian asked.

"I am."

She walked Sara up the aisle, feeling her sister right at her side. A tear trailed down her cheek. Sara paused at the end of the aisle and kissed her. "I love you, Aunt Lil."

"Love you, too, my dearest Sara."

Sara walked up to stand beside Noah, and she went to sit beside Gary in the front row of seats. He smiled at her and held her hand tightly, sharing this special day with her.

LILLIAN MINGLED with the guests at the reception, making sure everything ran smoothly and everyone felt welcome. She looked over at Sara and Noah standing at the end of the deck, surrounded by friends. She smiled when she saw Sara had the lace shawl draped over her shoulders. Her heart filled with joy. She'd never seen Sara so happy.

The fairy lights that Charlotte had placed around the deck illuminated just enough to make the scene look magical.

Lillian glanced down at the brilliant ring on her finger, sparkling in the light. Gary had bought the ring the afternoon after he'd come to talk to her and said he loved her. That very evening he'd taken her for a romantic beach walk and given her the ring with an official proposal. She smiled at the memory.

She looked up from staring at her ring and saw Camille and Delbert approaching. Delbert had a wide smile and Camille… didn't. Lillian pasted on a smile, unwilling to let Camille dampen her wonderful mood.

Delbert walked up and took her hand. "We were so glad to be included in this special day."

"Yes, it was, ah… *simple*. But I guess that's what Sara wanted." Camille gave a dismissive shrug.

"The wedding was spectacular. And Noah and Sara look happy, don't they?" Delbert glanced over at the couple.

"They might as well enjoy their couple time while they can." Camille's lips curved into a conspiratorial smile. "You know, until they have children."

Lillian gritted her teeth and just barely kept herself from telling Camille off. Luckily she was saved by Gary coming up right then and threading his arm around her. She leaned against him, glad to have him by her side.

"Delbert, Camille, nice to see you." Gary welcomed the couple.

"Good to see you, too. I hear congratulations are in order."

A wide smile spread across Gary's face at Delbert's words. "Thank you. I'm a very lucky man."

"That you are."

"I was so surprised to hear the news." Camille's eyes narrowed. "I mean, well, you know. At your age."

"Camille, darling. People fall in love at every age. Anyway, age is just a number." Delbert gently contradicted her.

"I guess. But... well. I still find it a bit unusual." Camille frowned with disapproval.

Delbert tossed her an apologetic look and turned to Camille. "Let's go say our congratulations to Noah and Sara."

They walked away and Gary laughed. "You did an admirable job of holding your tongue."

"That woman—" She took a deep breath. "But nothing can dampen my happiness right now."

Gary looked at her, his eyes full of love. "You look beautiful tonight."

"You don't look so bad yourself." She stared at this handsome man in front of her. The man who'd asked her to marry him. She glanced at her ring, then looked over at Sara and tears fell yet again.

Gary saw the tears and leaned close and whispered in her ear. "And our wedding is next."

She smiled at him through her happy tears. "In four short weeks."

DEAR READER, I hope you enjoyed Lillian and Gary's story… which continues in the next book! And what about Robin and Jay? Do they ever get their story? Download Book Five, Five Years or So, to find out!

As always, I appreciate my readers. Thanks so much for your support, and happy reading!

ALSO BY KAY CORRELL

THANK YOU for reading my story. I hope you enjoyed it. Sign up for my newsletter to be updated with information on new releases, promotions, give-aways, and newsletter-only surprises. The signup is at my website, kaycorrell.com.

Reviews help other readers find new books. I always appreciate when my readers take time to leave an honest review.

I love to hear from my readers. Feel free to contact me at authorcontact@kaycorrell.com

COMFORT CROSSING ~ THE SERIES

The Shop on Main - Book One

The Memory Box - Book Two

The Christmas Cottage - A Holiday Novella (Book 2.5)

The Letter - Book Three

The Christmas Scarf - A Holiday Novella (Book 3.5)

The Magnolia Cafe - Book Four

The Unexpected Wedding - Book Five

The Wedding in the Grove (crossover short story between series - Josephine and Paul from The Letter.)

LIGHTHOUSE POINT ~ THE SERIES

Wish Upon a Shell - Book One

Wedding on the Beach - Book Two

Love at the Lighthouse - Book Three

Cottage near the Point - Book Four

Return to the Island - Book Five

Bungalow by the Bay - Book Six

CHARMING INN ~ Return to Lighthouse Point

One Simple Wish - Book One

Two of a Kind - Book Two

Three Little Things - Book Three

Four Short Weeks - Book Four

Five Years or So - Book Five

Six Hours Away - Book Six

SWEET RIVER ~ THE SERIES

A Dream to Believe in - Book One

A Memory to Cherish - Book Two

A Song to Remember - Book Three

A Time to Forgive - Book Four

A Summer of Secrets - Book Five

A Moment in the Moonlight - Book Six

INDIGO BAY ~ Save by getting Kay's complete collection of stories previously published separately in the multi-author Indigo Bay series. The three stories are all interconnected.

Sweet Days by the Bay

Or buy them separately:

Sweet Sunrise - Book Three

Sweet Holiday Memories - A short holiday story

Sweet Starlight - Book Nine

ABOUT THE AUTHOR

Kay writes sweet, heartwarming stories that are a cross between women's fiction and contemporary romance. She is known for her charming small towns, quirky townsfolk, and enduring strong friendships between the women in her books.

Kay lives in the Midwest of the U.S. and can often be found out and about with her camera, taking a myriad of photographs which she likes to incorporate into her book covers. When not lost in her writing or photography, she can be found spending time with her ever-supportive husband, knitting, or playing with her puppies —two cavaliers and one naughty but adorable Australian shepherd. Kay and her husband also love to travel. When it comes to vacation time, she is torn between a nice trip to the beach or the mountains—but the mountains only get considered in the summer—she swears she's allergic to snow.

Learn more about Kay and her books at kaycorrell.com

While you're there, sign up for her newsletter to hear about new releases, sales, and giveaways.

WHERE TO FIND ME:
kaycorrell.com
authorcontact@kaycorrell.com

Join my Facebook Reader Group. We have lots of fun and you'll hear about sales and new releases first!
https://www.facebook.com/groups/KayCorrell/

facebook.com/KayCorrellAuthor

instagram.com/kaycorrell

pinterest.com/kaycorrellauthor

amazon.com/author/kaycorrell

bookbub.com/authors/kay-correll

Made in the USA
Middletown, DE
07 July 2025

10219444R00170